SHAWNEE SETTLERS

Elizabeth Bradley—Widowed in genteel Virginia, she was forced to come West. Now she has to choose between a suave man of wealth, who'll take her back to the East, and a rugged man of action, who's at home with the harsh realities of an untamed land.

Tim Ryan—He fought to establish his thriving ranch near Shawnee. Can he now fight against his neighbors? Can he fight against his feelings for Elizabeth Bradley—who resembles the wife who betrayed him?

George Bigelow—He knows he's going places, no matter who has to die. And he knows Elizabeth will go with him—whether she likes it or not.

Meg Callahan—She runs a "parlor house" with the prettiest girls in town. She can have most any man she wants, but the man she wants most is Tim Ryan.

Black Wolf—As a beleaguered Sioux chief he has two alternatives: make war on the whites and die, or watch his starving people die.

The Stagecoach Series
Ask your bookseller for the books you have missed

STAGECOACH STATION 37:
SHAWNEE

Hank Mitchum

Created by the producers of
**Wagons West, White Indian,
Badge,** and **America 2040.**

Book Creations Inc., Canaan. NY · Lyle Kenyon Engel. Founder

BANTAM BOOKS
TORONTO · NEW YORK · LONDON · SYDNEY · AUCKLAND

STAGECOACH STATION 37: SHAWNEE

A Bantam Book / published by arrangement with
Book Creations, Inc.

Bantam edition / September 1988

Produced by Book Creations, Inc.
Lyle Kenyon Engel, Founder

ISBN 0-553-27404-X

Published simultaneously in the United States and Canada

Bantam Books are published by Bantam Books, a division of Bantam
Doubleday Dell Publishing Group, Inc. Its trademark, consisting of
the words "Bantam Books" and the portrayal of a rooster, is
Registered in U.S. Patent and Trademark Office and in other
countries. Marca Registrada. Bantam Books, 666 Fifth Avenue,
New York, New York 10103.

PRINTED IN THE UNITED STATES OF AMERICA

KR   0 9 8 7 6 5 4 3 2 1

STAGECOACH STATION 37:
SHAWNEE

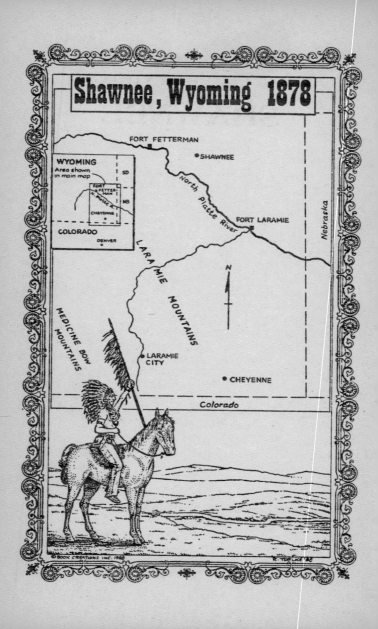

Chapter One

Lurching around a bend, the engine shrieked and belched a cloud of black soot. "Cheyenne, Wyoming!" a voice bellowed. It was eight o'clock in the morning, and Elizabeth Bradley winced as the momentum flung her nine-year-old son, Charlie, against her like a sack of bricks. Charlie could sleep anywhere.

Pushing Charlie upright, Elizabeth brushed a blonde fringe of hair away from her face and took off her black bonnet to poke hairpins back into the knot on the top of her head. She suspected that her hair, like the rest of her, was more sooty gray than blonde from the dirt and ash that came through the open windows. The journey on the steam cars from Virginia to Omaha, and now west to Cheyenne, had left her aching and gritty from head to toe. From Cheyenne she would take the stagecoach north to Shawnee, where a job awaited her as housekeeper to a cattle rancher named Timothy Ryan. He was going to pay her twenty dollars a month—more than she had ever made at home by ruining her eyes over fine needlework and trying to cling to a way of life that, before she was sixteen, had been lost to the Civil War. A new life, a new country—anything was possible in the West, or so her friend Mattie Ferris had said. Despite the grinding journey, Elizabeth was glad Mattie had talked her into it.

She took a silver-backed hand mirror from her carpet-bag and peered into it. A pale heart-shaped face with

1

china-blue eyes under long gold lashes looked back at her. She hoped Mr. Ryan did not think she looked too young. His sister, Mattie, had not seemed to think so, but then Mattie knew that Elizabeth was twenty-six. The black clothes and bonnet with its yard of widow's veiling made her look older, too.

"You'll do fine," Mattie had said briskly, pouring her a cup of tea and patting Elizabeth's hand awkwardly with hers. "It's a good thing you're young enough to start a new life, and not turn into an old trout like me with nothing to do but snub Yankees and try to pretend we still have money when we don't. My brother needs a housekeeper badly—those girls of his must be running wild since his wife died. And you'll do better in a place where everything doesn't remind you of poor Charles."

"Yes, I suppose I will," Elizabeth had said politely, silently wishing she could mourn her late husband more wholeheartedly.

She had known a year after she married Charles Bradley that it had been a mistake. After the war there had been so few men left to marry, but at sixteen one had to marry someone. Charles had sulked over his family's lost glory and then had invested wildly in speculation, attempting to regain their vanished fortune. In the end, against Elizabeth's wishes and advice, he had managed to lose what little they had left. When he died four years ago, in 1874, Elizabeth found herself with no inheritance, just a house on which she could not pay the taxes and little Charlie to compensate for her mistake. After selling the house, she had taken rooms in a boardinghouse and tried to make the house money last by doing fine sewing. That had not worked very well, and she had been desperate when Mattie put her proposition to her.

"Tim went and married a North Carolina girl after the war," Mattie had said with exasperation. "Now that she's gone, he's got seven-year-old twin girls, and not a soul to look after them but a cook who's already got her hands full. He needs a housekeeper whether he thinks so or not."

"You mean he doesn't think so?" Elizabeth said, taken

aback at Mattie's cheerful manipulation of her brother's domestic life.

"You write to him," Mattie said. "He'll change his tune when he sees you're a sensible woman. His wife—well, Caroline was delicate. She didn't stand up to Wyoming very well. Tim's done better for himself since then." Mattie peered shrewdly at Elizabeth over her rimless spectacles. "In any case, I suspect you've got more backbone than poor Caroline had."

Elizabeth hoped so, since she had written to Mr. Ryan, trying to make herself sound as elderly and capable as she could—thirty-eight at least—and he had written back, sending her a train ticket and money for the stagecoach.

Now she was nearly there. The train ground to a halt at Cheyenne with a shriek of whistles and a cloud of hot steam and ash. Charlie was awake and wide-eyed again— his pale hair sooty and tousled, his black jacket and knickers travel stained and torn at the knees, and his high-button boots looking as if he had stolen them from a tramp. Yet his round face was alive with excitement. This was an adventure!

The strange people on the steam cars, the endless prairie that had unfolded before them after they crossed the Mississippi, the time that the engineer had stopped the train because a frantic rider had flagged them down to say that Indians had cut the rails ten miles ahead—all were adventure to Charlie. He had slept only when he was too tired to look out the windows any longer, or when it was too dark to see. He had eaten ravenously of the same unending fare served at all the meal stops along the way, and he had asked incessant questions of any adult willing to answer them.

Elizabeth picked up her carpetbag and stood up, taking Charlie by the hand to disembark before the other passengers filled the aisle.

"Mama!" Charlie's voice rose to an excited shriek as they made their way to the open doors.

A half-dozen men appeared on the platform below them. They wore high-heeled boots, woolen trousers slung low on their hips, flannel shirts, vests, bandannas, and the broad-brimmed hats that westerners seemed to wear everywhere, even when they sat down to eat. They carried carpetbags, battered leather satchels, or just a blanket rolled up under one arm. Two had saddles slung over their shoulders. All of them, Elizabeth noted uneasily, had revolvers.

"Cowboys!" Charlie cried happily.

Elizabeth pulled Charlie closer to her and tried not to stare at them, uncomfortably aware that they were staring at her. In the stories that circulated in the East, the cowboy was a menacing creature: quick with a gun, unheeding of the law, and dangerous to an unprotected woman. She had always taken most of those tales with a grain of salt, but they came unpleasantly back to her now.

"Purty, ain't she?" one of them said in an audible voice. And another called up to her, "Stayin' in Cheyenne, lady? Kin I show you around?" Two of them were passing a bottle back and forth.

"Shut up, Texas, and leave the lady alone. You're scaring her," another voice said, and Elizabeth turned to see that it was the tall, dapper-looking man who had been sitting across the aisle from them. He stood beside her, also waiting to descend.

Elizabeth held her head up determinedly, grateful now for the dowdy high-necked dress and the widow's black veiling. Ignoring the cowboys, she stared across the platform at the weatherbeaten depot and water tower of Cheyenne, waiting for the cowboys to move out of the way. A few longhorn cattle milled in the stockyards beyond the tracks, and behind the depot she could see the tall false fronts of buildings along the muddy main street. Even over the noise of the railroad yard she could hear whoops and gunfire that she supposed must be coming from the saloons, but the occupants of the wagons and buggies jamming the street seemed to take no notice of the noises.

Suddenly there was a gasp from a thin nervous man with a handlebar mustache who had occupied a seat two rows behind her. With horror, Elizabeth saw three cowboys running toward the tracks, dragging a limp form with a noose around its neck. They threw the rope over the crossbar of a telegraph pole and hauled on it. A woman in the aisle shrieked.

As the swaying figure rose, one of the lynch mob drew his revolver and fired point-blank at the dangling man. Elizabeth put her hand over Charlie's eyes amid shouts of maniacal laughter from the cowboys.

The man with the handlebar mustache was trying frantically to clamber past the luggage in the aisle, shouting, "This is the territorial capital! This is outrageous! Where is the law in Wyoming? I shall telegraph to Washington at once!"

"Won't do no good," one of the cowboys said lazily. "Reckon he's dead by now."

Elizabeth turned away from the scene with such horror in her face that the dapper man beside her took pity on her.

"Simmer down, bud," he said to the thin man, pushing him back into his seat. "It's all right, ma'am. They're only putting on a show for you."

"A—a show?" Elizabeth looked at the hanged man with sudden suspicion and took her hand from Charlie's eyes. He wiggled indignantly to the edge of the steps and hung half over them, with Elizabeth clinging to his hand.

"It's straw, Mama!" He pointed gleefully at the wisps drifting from the bullet-riddled shirt.

"Yes, I see it is." Elizabeth turned a frosty gaze on the laughing cowboys below her. Suddenly they did not look so menacing, and she saw that most of them could not be older than eighteen.

"You should be ashamed of yourselves," she said severely.

"You must forgive them, ma'am," said the dapper-looking man standing beside her. "It's only high spirits."

"And cheap whiskey," Elizabeth said tartly, but her lips were beginning to curl into a smile.

As her fear of the cowboys abated, she took stock of her traveling companion. He appeared to be about forty, with a handsome, urbane face, neatly trimmed side-whiskers, and a prosperous air. He wore high-heeled boots and a broad-brimmed felt hat like the cowboys, but his gray woolen trousers were neatly pressed, and instead of a vest and flannel shirt, he wore a gray sack coat, stiff collar, and four-in-hand tie. He looked almost like an easterner, but not quite.

"Does this sort of thing go on all the time?" Elizabeth asked.

"Not once the roundup season starts," her companion said with a smile. "These boys are all heading for work on the ranches during the spring branding. A lot of them probably on my ranch," he added, pitching his voice a little louder, "so they had better behave."

His words sobered the cowboys on the platform, and they moved away, allowing the passengers to descend.

"My name is George Bigelow," the man said, helping Elizabeth down. He bowed politely. "I own the Double X spread, just outside Shawnee."

"I am Elizabeth Bradley," Elizabeth said. She held out her hand. "And this is my son, Charlie."

"May I ask where you're headed?"

"Shawnee, too," Elizabeth said. "I'm going to be house-keeper for Mr. Timothy Ryan. Perhaps you know him?"

George Bigelow's eyebrows rose briefly. He looked her over with a smile, a scrutiny that was a little too personal to be proper. "Yes, Ryan and I are old acquaintances."

There was something in his voice that made Elizabeth guess that Mr. Ryan was an acquaintance he could do without. She looked at him uncertainly.

Bigelow smiled and motioned her to the end of the platform, where a small, frame building stood with a dusty stagecoach waiting outside it.

"If you'll allow me, ma'am," Bigelow offered, "I'll see to your ticket for you, and make sure your trunk's been unloaded. Sometimes they go straight on to California if nobody stops them."

"That's kind of you," Elizabeth said as she gave him her ticket money gratefully. While Bigelow was in the depot, she inspected the stagecoach. It was a big Concord coach, with a luggage boot behind, and more luggage strapped on top. The driver, his hat down over his eyes, appeared to be asleep until he spat a stream of tobacco juice into the dust beside the left wheel. As she watched, another man climbed up beside him and settled down with a shotgun across his lap.

Mercy, Elizabeth thought.

Charlie, however, appeared to have no misgivings as he

eyed the stage. When George Bigelow reappeared and helped Elizabeth into the coach, Charlie bounced up beside her, his eyes eager. He looked around the dim, dusty interior with satisfaction and settled at his mother's left, next to the window.

"I'll be charmed to welcome you to Shawnee, Mrs. Bradley," Bigelow said, sitting beside her on her right. "I do trust you won't find us too wild when you get to know us."

Elizabeth looked over Charlie's head and out the window at the cowboys. They were no worse than the young soldiers she had tended in Richmond Hospital. "No, I think I'm going to enjoy Wyoming, Mr. Bigelow." She smiled at him, and Bigelow smiled back, genially conspiratorial.

"I do trust you will think of me as a friend and call upon me if ever you need help."

Elizabeth's smile faded a little in uncertainty. Why did Bigelow think she might need help? Was there something about Mr. Ryan she should know?

Before she could speculate further, a party of three women got on board and settled down across from them, just as the stage lurched into motion.

"Mama, look at the lady with all the birds on her hat!" Charlie whispered in awe.

"Hush, Charlie, and don't point," Elizabeth whispered back, but her eyes were opened wide. The eldest of the three women was somewhere in her forties, but her pretty, if timeworn, face was made more youthful by rouge and face powder. Elizabeth had never known a woman who actually painted her face, and she wondered if the woman's hair was dyed, too. But the clothes! The dress was of strawberry-colored satin, had an enormous bustle, and was adorned with bows and pockets of black lace and velvet. Elizabeth had not had a new dress in nearly six years. She knew she ought not even to look at a woman like that, but she could not resist. On the woman's feet were red kid high-heeled boots, and at her throat was a frill that Elizabeth wistfully recognized as real French lace. A red hat surmounted by three teal-blue birds rested elegantly on her head. She was accompanied by two younger women, equally fashionably dressed and laden with bandboxes and parcels.

"Mama, who are those ladies?" Charlie demanded.

"I don't know," Elizabeth said, but she thought she did. She turned Charlie around firmly. "Look out the window."

"I dunno why I couldn'ta had that green taffeta yesterday," one of the girls was complaining loudly. "You let Sadie buy some of it. I'm tired of blue!"

"Green just isn't your color, Lucy, and that's a fact," the older woman said.

"You'd look just like a old yellow wax candle in my green," a plump, pink-cheeked woman with soft brown hair said.

The sallow-skinned Lucy stuck out her tongue at her. "At least I'm not so fat it takes three people to lace up my stays!"

"That's enough! You'll both behave ladylike or I won't take you again." The woman with the birds on her hat gave her brood a sharp glance. "And I won't have you talking to cowboys in the street anymore, either," she added. "My girls don't receive callers on a public platform. Haven't I knocked any refinement into you yet?"

Elizabeth looked straight ahead, her ears burning, as the girls dutifully compared their purchases.

George Bigelow watched Tim Ryan's little housekeeper with amusement. He supposed she had never seen the inhabitants of a parlor house—the polite euphemism for a whorehouse—up close before, but it would be hard to mistake Meg Callahan and her girls for anything else. Elizabeth Bradley was a beautiful woman, Bigelow thought, even in that dreadful black dress, which his experienced eye told him had been "turned" once, taken apart and put back together with the inner side of the fabric out, when the outer side had become worn. Not much money, but her soft southern speech had a lady's accent. Certainly not much money if she was willing to come West and keep house for Tim Ryan.

Emma Lang leaned her hoe against the porch railing and sat down on a wooden apple crate just to look at the new fence line that Monty had strung and the good, solid barn they had built. She and Monty were making a home out of nothing here on the prairie, and it seemed to Emma that she ought to just sit and appreciate it once in a while. Time to appreciate did not come all that often.

Emma arched her back, easing her aching shoulder muscles. Off beyond the corral, there was a new-turned garden plot. She had plowed it, dug out all the weeds and prairie grass, and planted it herself.

It was beautiful, Emma thought, all that naked earth full of corn, beans, squash, even melons, waiting to grow.

Out on the prairie, beyond the circle of her barn and house and garden, she could hear the lowing of longhorn cattle. All the ranch hands from the big spreads were out spotting cattle, seeing where they were bunched up, before the start of the spring roundup. Most people out here paid attention to nothing but cattle, Emma thought. Even Monty, trying to build up their herd, had not helped her a bit with their garden. Monty would do his appreciating when there were canned beans and melon pickles on the table this winter, she knew.

Emma stretched. There was the wash to do, and supper to start yet, but she thought she would just sit here for a few more minutes and look at the garden.

The nearby lowing of cattle made her lift her head with a start. Three men were herding a dozen longhorns past; the cattle milled in a bunch, lowing, as they came up against Monty's new fence. That was not Monty.

"Goddamn squatters!" One of the cowboys leaned down from his horse and cut the fence, pushing the cattle through the gap.

Emma stood up and ran across the yard, furious. "You turn those cows back!" she called to them. "This is our land."

The cowboy looked at her under his hat brim as the cattle moved past. "This is free range, girlie," he told her. "You tell your pa we said so."

Emma pushed her sunbonnet back from her face. "My pa's not here. I'm Mrs. Monty Lang, and this is our land, homesteaded legal."

The cowboy hooted scornfully. "I heard Lang had married some farmer's baby, but I thought she'd be bigger'n nine years old."

"I'm sixteen," Emma said angrily.

The cowboy looked at her closely, and Emma flushed. "Doggone if you ain't," he said.

"Get off our land!"

"You'll be lucky if all we do's cut a little fence," the cowboy said lazily. "Seein' as you're sixteen." He yipped at the cattle, and they broke into a trot through the yard.

Emma ran after them. "You got no right! I know where you come from. I saw the brand on them cows. Get 'em off my land or I'll complain to the law about you."

The cowboy wheeled his horse to a stop and spun it around. "I ain't got time to waste on no farmer's brat. You want something to complain about, I can handle that." He spied the newly planted garden, kicked his horse up, and drove the cattle into it.

"No!" Emma ran after him, choking in the dust. "That's new planted!"

"Well, now it ain't." The cattle lumbered through the soft earth. When they reached the other side, the cowboys, laughing, turned them back through it, again and again.

"Stop it!" The dust rose in clouds around Emma, gagging her, clinging to the tears on her cheeks.

When the garden was trampled into ruins, the cowboys drove the cattle from it, cutting another piece of fence, leaving Emma sobbing in the dusty wreckage.

When the last cow had lumbered through the fence, the cowboy turned to Emma again. "You tell your husband not to string no more fence," he said. "We don't allow squatter fence here."

As the heavy-footed cattle moved away across the open prairie, Emma sat down in the dirt, weeping, picking up the crushed and scattered seeds that had been three days' work.

The yard outside the barn on Tim Ryan's ranch was splotched with melting snow, and bootheels and ponies' hooves had churned it into muddy slush. Inside the barn,

Tim Ryan smacked a big bay named Jericho on the flank to make him move over, and the horse looked at him reproachfully. Unlike the cow ponies, which would have kicked a buggy to pieces, Jericho was a horse of much dignity. As Ryan tightened the harness straps, John Potter, foreman of the Broken R Ranch, stuck his head in the barn door.

"We need salt, sugar, and a keg of nails. Probably a passel of other things," John said. "You might take the wagon."

"Naw, that poor old lady's been bounced around enough on the stage. I can't make her ride all the way back here in a buckboard. I'll put in an order at Fishburn's, and you can pick it up tomorrow."

"You're mighty solicitous for a man who swore he didn't want a housekeeper in the first place," John commented.

Tim Ryan grinned at him. He picked up the hat that Jericho had nudged off his head and jammed it down over his black hair. "Natural reaction to my sister Mattie," he said. "Mattie's always been a sight too ready to tell me what I need. Comes of being the oldest. But after the woman wrote to me, I had to admit she sounded pretty good, and God knows those little devils need a lady to take them in hand. They're starting to swear like cowhands. I put Susannah over my knee this morning because she called her sister a very bad word." Ryan's tone was exaggeratedly solemn, and his green eyes looked amused.

John Potter laughed.

"I said I was sorry, Pa. Can't we go, too?" The twins appeared behind John Potter in the doorway, Susannah doing her best to look contrite. They were dark haired like their father, with light blue eyes and pretty, impish faces. Carrie held a chicken, which she was determinedly trying to tame, under one arm. The chicken did not look as if it liked the training, and it had not improved Carrie's pinafore.

"That's 'Papa,' not 'Pa,' " Ryan said automatically, but he knew it was not going to take. His own educated speech had slipped since he had come West, and the girls were never going to learn to speak properly without a better example.

"No, she's had a rough enough trip without you two

pestering her right off. There's no room in the buggy for
you, anyway. She's got her son with her, and she's bound
to have a trunk. But you can stay up and have dinner with
us when we get back." The normal dinner hour at the
Broken R was five o'clock, but they would not get back
from town till after eight, and Mrs. Bradley was bound to
be hungry.

Ryan bent down and kissed each girl in turn. A suggestion that he kiss the chicken was declined.

As Susannah dragged Carrie from the barn, Tim Ryan
gave his foreman a thoughtful look. "Better saddle a horse
and come along. You can take her son up with you if you
have to. No telling how much stuff she's brought along."

No telling anything, he thought as he led Jericho out of
the barn. From the letter she had written, Elizabeth
Bradley did not sound like the delicate type, but if she
was, she would not last long out here.

The Broken R was the second-largest ranch in the county,
next to George Bigelow's, and it boasted a two-story ranch
house, painted white, with a veranda around three sides.
Civilization left off about a hundred yards away, just beyond
the bunkhouse. There the longhorn cattle that roamed
freely over the prairie and hills were rounded up only
twice a year—in the spring for branding and in the fall to
sell off the young steers. The nearest town, Shawnee, was
ten miles away, and it was a far cry from the neat, tree-
lined towns of the East.

As Jericho pulled the buggy toward Shawnee, Tim Ryan
thought back to when he had first come to Wyoming.

When he was eighteen, Ryan had gone west to Texas
from North Carolina out of sheer boredom. He had worked
on some of the ranches there, punching cows and occasionally breaking saddle horses for the ranch owners. When
the Civil War had broken out, he went home to fight, and
at the end of those terrible years, he returned to Texas
with nothing more than a pair of Confederate-issue army
boots and a ragged uniform. But in Texas he had pros-
pered, rounding up the wild longhorns that had run un-
tended and unclaimed on the open range during the war
years and trailing them north to Wyoming, where he
bought some acreage about twenty miles east of Fort

Fetterman and started to build a ranch. Two years later, when he left for a visit with his sister in North Carolina, the Broken R Ranch was a simple sod house and three hundred head of longhorns, but it looked very fine to Tim Ryan, who had fallen in love with the wild Wyoming country.

During that visit to North Carolina, his sister Mattie and his middle sister Annalee had introduced him to Caroline Ashbury. Caroline was everything that Tim Ryan could want: blonde, delicate, with bright blue eyes like clear water, and heart-stoppingly beautiful. Tim Ryan had fallen instantly in love.

Caroline Ashbury, wearing her one good gown, had set herself to charm Annalee Ryan's Wyoming brother, who talked so grandly about his ranch there. Everyone at home was poor then, and of the four men courting Caroline, three were old and one had lost a leg in the war. Caroline wanted none of them. She wanted Tim Ryan and his Wyoming ranch, and she got him—and then got a terrible surprise when she actually saw the ranch that was her husband's pride.

The Broken R in those days had not looked much better than Montana Lang's place did now, Tim Ryan thought as they neared the track that led off toward Monty's spread. Monty had been a ranch hand of Ryan's before he had fallen in love with little Emma and struck out on his own. Now Monty had a good piece of creek land between Ryan's place and George Bigelow's and was exhausting himself working his spread into shape.

As they got closer to Monty's land, Ryan narrowed his eyes. "Hold on a minute," he told John Potter.

Monty Lang was out in the yard with Emma, who was sitting in the dirt, scratching for something and crying. As Ryan got closer, he saw that a piece of fence was down.

Ryan turned the buggy toward the house, and John Potter followed him. "You need a hand with something?" Ryan called, and then he spotted the wreckage of Emma's garden. "What happened?"

"Bigelow's hands turned a dozen head of cattle through Emma's garden," Monty said. He tugged at Emma. "Get up. You ain't gonna find those seeds."

Emma wiped a dirty hand across her tear-streaked face, but she did not stand up.

"Did they damage anything else?" Ryan said.

"Not this time," Monty said grimly. "But I don't like leaving Emma alone after this."

"They didn't hurt me," Emma sobbed.

"I don't like taking any chances," Monty said. "I told you this was coming, Tim. It's gonna be open season on homesteaders if the big cattlemen have their way."

"Not all of them," Ryan said. "Just Bigelow, and you know how I feel about him. No one else would do this just for spite."

"It wasn't even Bigelow himself. It was three of his hands," Monty said. "There's more bad feeling than you know."

"Bigelow's hands take their cue from him," Ryan said, as he looked uncomfortably at the trampled garden. "But I can't believe even George Bigelow would deliberately send them to do this. Cut fence, yeah, but not this. They just got above themselves."

"You got your head in the sand, Tim," Monty said. "You're a cattleman yourself. You know what the feeling is."

Ryan sighed. "There's a lot of talk against fencing, I know that. I don't much like fence myself. But as long as it's legal, I'm not going to fight it. And I don't believe the other ranch owners will either, outside of a law court."

"I gotta have the fence," Monty cried. "I haven't got but fifteen head. I turn 'em loose all year, I won't see 'em again."

"I turned mine loose when I was starting," Ryan said, "with not many more than you got now."

"And there wasn't another spread within fifty miles of yours, either," Monty argued. "Now there're a dozen big ones, all thinking the public land belongs to them and determined they're gonna keep it that way. I turn my stock loose, how many of them do you think I'm gonna get back out of the spring roundup?"

Ryan could not argue that point. That was the hell of it with this fence question—everyone was right.

"I don't know," he said. "But I don't think anyone but

Bigelow would stoop to this. And I don't think he'll go any further." He tried to sound convincing, but he wished he were that sure. Yet it would not do any good to scare Emma more than she already was.

"We'll see," was all Monty said. He knelt down and put an arm around Emma. "Come on, honey. Get up now."

When Ryan had turned the buggy back down the road to Shawnee, he looked over his shoulder at Monty and Emma. They were standing in the garden, Emma leaning against Monty's shoulder. *Poor kid*, Ryan thought. But they would do all right. In the long run, they would do just fine. Monty was lucky. Emma Lang loved the land the way her husband did. *If Caroline had just loved our land like that* . . . , Ryan thought wistfully. His mouth twisted bitterly. *Ah, damn.*

Tim Ryan put his rebellious, unhappy wife out of his mind and spurred Jericho toward Shawnee.

The stage lurched into Shawnee in a cloud of dust. Elizabeth, aching and stiff from the eight-hour ride, straightened Charlie's jacket and picked up her carpetbag. George Bigelow gallantly stepped down from the stagecoach door ahead of her and then helped her disembark. She climbed down the steps, clutching Charlie, who had a tendency to explore if no one kept a grip on him, and stared around her, feeling overwhelmed by the space. Beyond the wooden stage depot, Elizabeth could see the main street of Shawnee, edged with boardwalks. Beyond that was nothing, only rolling grassland and some hills in the distance, with the beautiful, snow-covered sweep of the Rocky Mountains to the west. She looked up to find George Bigelow smiling down at her.

"You get used to it after a while. Doesn't seem so unsettling then. Your trunk's been unloaded—I checked."

"Thank you so much. You've been very kind."

Bigelow lifted his hat with a graceful bow. "I hope you like Wyoming, Mrs. Bradley. And I hope to be seeing you again."

"I do hope so, Mr. Bigelow." Elizabeth gave him her hand.

"You take care of yourself, young man." He ruffled Charlie's hair, and Charlie gave him a baleful look. Bigelow smiled at Elizabeth. "And remember, if you need assistance of any kind, you have only to call on me." He raised his hat again and departed. Apparently he was not going to stay to introduce her to Timothy Ryan.

Elizabeth scanned the street for someone who might be Mr. Ryan. A dark-haired man in an open buggy seemed to be looking for someone. Elizabeth took Charlie in one hand and her carpetbag in the other and went to see. The dark-haired man raised his hat as she approached and regarded her warily. He had green eyes in a tanned, fine-boned, clean-shaven face, a wide, attractive mouth, and long-fingered hands. He was the most alive-looking man Elizabeth had ever seen. There might be humor in that dark face somewhere, Elizabeth thought, but at the moment it regarded her with stony disapproval.

Elizabeth felt herself bristling. "I am looking for Mr. Timothy Ryan," she informed him.

The dark man in the buggy narrowed his green eyes at her. "I'm Timothy Ryan," he said. "God help us, don't tell me you're Mrs. Bradley."

Chapter Two

Tim Ryan inspected his new housekeeper with something between despair and fury. *Damn and blast that meddling Mattie anyway!* Mattie was going to get a letter that would steam the curl right out of her false fringe. As for that lying Mrs. Bradley—a capable widow woman indeed!

Cornflower-blue eyes looked back at him under arching light brown brows, and that awful black bonnet could not quite conceal an aureole of gold curls. *I'll bet she was the belle of four counties*, Ryan thought grimly. His physical reaction to the woman standing by the buggy was almost overpowering—the same reaction he had always had to Caroline—and he suppressed it ruthlessly. The last thing in the world he wanted was another woman like his former wife.

"I am Elizabeth Bradley," she said with a touch of hauteur, "and this is my son, Charlie."

This isn't going to do at all, Elizabeth thought. *He's much too young. This isn't respectable. Mattie must have been mad.* She had just assumed that he was near Mattie's age. How was the irritable Mr. Ryan going to like it when she asked him for railroad fare back to Virginia?

She was steeling herself to do so when he said curtly, "Well, you're younger than I expected. My sister must have lost her mind!"

Elizabeth balked at this echo of her own conclusions.

17

His soft North Carolina drawl was overlaid with a western cadence that would have been pleasant to the ear had it not been so tinged with acid.

"Here's your trunk, ma'am." A big man with a round, friendly face swung her trunk off his shoulder and into the back of the buggy. "Glad to have you with us."

"This is my foreman, John Potter," Ryan said. "I don't think Mrs. Bradley's gonna be staying after all," he added to the foreman.

Elizabeth glared at him. She was so tired; she wanted to take her stays off and sleep for a week. The prospect of retracing that brutal journey was almost more than she could bear. But she could not bring herself to slink away like a schoolgirl in front of Tim Ryan and his foreman.

"I am twenty-six," she announced firmly, looking Ryan in the eye. "Surely that is old enough to manage a house and children, Mr. Ryan. I have been doing so since I was sixteen. How old did you think I was? I did tell you I had a nine-year-old son."

"You didn't tell me you'd got started on it so early," Ryan said, but his voice was less acid. "You're gonna get talked about, you know. It doesn't look halfway respectable."

"I thought you had a woman to cook for you, Mr. Ryan. Surely with another woman for a chaperone . . . ?"

Ryan grinned at her, lighting up his dark face with the humor that Elizabeth had suspected earlier. "Oh, yeah, I have a cook."

Behind her, John Potter opened his mouth to say something, and Ryan shook his head at him. John closed it again, but he gave his boss a dubious look.

"Well, if you're that determined, Mrs. Bradley, I guess you can have the job," Ryan was saying. "I got to admit I need you. But don't blame me when all the old hens in town start clucking about it."

"I'm sure there will be no gossip once they understand that I am here to work." She was not sure of that at all, but she was not going to admit it.

As Ryan leaned down from the buggy to help her in, Elizabeth was very conscious of his hands on hers, and the smile in his cat-green eyes. If there were to be no talk, she thought ruefully, she would have to be careful. Tim

Ryan stirred a spark in her somewhere that she had not felt before, certainly not with Charles. But she would die before she admitted it. She called to Charlie, who had drifted off.

"Take him up with you," Ryan called to John Potter after eyeing the cramped space in the back of the buggy. Elizabeth's trunk and carpetbag took up most of it.

Charlie, eyes round with excitement, let himself be hauled up behind the saddle on John Potter's bay. Like the buggy horse, the bay carried the Broken R brand on its flank.

Ryan took the buggy whip from its socket. "I tell you what, Mrs. Bradley. We'll give it six months and see how we do. Either one of us can back out then, with no hard feelings. How's that?"

"That's very reasonable of you, Mr. Ryan," Elizabeth said sweetly.

As he shook out Jericho's reins, Tim Ryan was uncomfortably aware of her nearness. He was torn between a desire to know what she looked like without that black bonnet and a wish that he had had John Potter drive instead. Elizabeth Bradley was an unsettling woman to sit next to, he decided as they drove away from the depot.

They stopped outside Fishburn's General Store so that Ryan could place an order for John Potter to pick up the next day, and while he was inside, Elizabeth took her first close look at Shawnee. The main street leading from the depot was two blocks long, flanked by weathered boardwalks. Across from Fishburn's was a two-story building with a painted sign identifying it as the Sawyer House Hotel. There were two doors on the first floor, one apparently leading to the lobby. As Elizabeth watched, the other door swung open, revealing a long mahogany bar with a mirror behind it. A few men were leaning against it, their feet resting on the brass rail that ran along the bottom.

Beyond the stage depot behind Elizabeth was a scattering of cruder buildings and tents. She could hear the faint notes of a piano coming from one of those buildings.

Tim Ryan came out of Fishburn's, and they continued down the main street, northward from the depot. Beyond

Fishburn's were a law office with gilt lettering on the door, the sheriff's office and jail, and a tall building with a cupola on top that Tim Ryan said was the town hall. At the end of the block, Main Street abruptly became a narrow track. A few white frame houses with trees in the yard lined the side streets that crossed the track. At the edge of town stood the schoolhouse, painted red with a brass bell on a post in the dirt yard, and the plain, graceful white structure of St. Peter's Church of the Prairie. Beyond these last buildings, the rolling sweep of grassland and the mountains in the distance spread before them.

As they traveled toward the Broken R, they passed a few sod houses of homesteaders. Tim Ryan pointed to a distant cluster of buildings that he said belonged to old Dad Henry, who, Ryan claimed, should know better than to try ranching at his age.

"I met a man on the train," Elizabeth said. "A very pleasant man named George Bigelow. He said he knew you."

"Hmph," responded Ryan, and Elizabeth decided not to pursue that any further.

"It's immense," she said after a moment, watching the shadows fade into dusk across the tall grass.

"Does it scare you?" Ryan asked.

"I think it does."

"It oughta," he said knowingly. "A good healthy respect for the land is what makes a survivor out here."

"Are there Indians?" she asked, looking at the Winchester on the floor at her feet.

"There're Indians pretty much anywhere out here," he said with a faint note of evasion in his voice. "Now don't start thinking you're gonna be scalped in your bed. They're peaceful right now, and the tribes are supposed to stay on their own lands to the north. Besides, if anyone gets attacked, it's always the little settlers, the small homesteaders' spreads that are too isolated."

"Mr. Ryan," Elizabeth inquired faintly, "is that supposed to be a comfort?"

Ryan burst out laughing. "I guess it doesn't sound comforting at that. But you'll be safe on the Broken R. I wouldn't have my kids out here if I didn't think so. Besides, one of the local chiefs is a friend of mine. I'll be warned if there's trouble coming." He did not sound as if he thought that was impossible.

"What makes a man come out here?" Elizabeth asked, curious, since Ryan seemed willing to talk.

"Well, for the cattlemen it's the grass mainly. It's good feed for longhorns, and as long as the land stays open, we can drive 'em clear to Omaha before we have to ship by rail. It's cheaper that way. We sell a lot of beef in San Francisco, too."

"I didn't mean that exactly," Elizabeth said. "I suppose I meant—why come West at all?"

"I thought you did," Ryan said, "but that one's hard to answer. It's easier to spout a lot of figures about so many head per acre, and profit on the dollar, and so on. A lot of the cattlemen who think only about making money don't live here at all. They hire a foreman to run the place. Bigelow will be one of those in a year or two. But the ones who come to live—mostly I think we come looking for something, or running from something. Sometimes maybe both. Same as you."

Elizabeth started to deny that she was running from anything, but stopped when she realized Ryan was right. "I wonder if a sense of adventure always boils down to sheer desperation," she said thoughtfully.

"Well, a wandering foot, anyway," Ryan said. "Sometimes that's the same thing." He peered at her pale face and determined chin through the gathering dark. "I believe you're gonna make it, Mrs. Bradley."

Evening shadows had turned gently into night in the two hours it took them to reach the Broken R. The glow of lamps lighting the first floor of the ranch house greeted them as Ryan pulled the buggy up to the veranda. Elizabeth gratefully let Ryan lift her down, aware of his hands around her waist. She staggered a little as she hit the ground.

Laced up like a beetle in a shell, like all women, Ryan thought. "You ought to take those stays off and let yourself breathe a little," he said, with no apparent regard for convention. Women's underwear was not a mentionable subject.

Charlie, exhausted by all the excitement, was sound asleep behind John Potter. Ryan lifted him down and carried him up the steps, leaving Elizabeth to bring her carpetbag and John Potter the trunk.

At a shout from Ryan, two ranch hands appeared and led the horses off. They tipped their hats politely to Elizabeth, peering at her by the light of a lantern. As they vanished into the dark, Elizabeth heard one of them hoot softly and say, "She sure is good-lookin' for a poor old widder woman!"

By Wyoming standards, Tim Ryan's ranch house was luxurious. He had built it with the first real money he had made. Inside the front door a hallstand with two pairs of steer horns for hooks stood against the wall. It had a seat at the base of it and was backed by a mirror.

In the dim lamplight Elizabeth caught a glimpse of a hollow-eyed and depressed-looking woman in the mirror. *A year is long enough,* she thought, startled at her appearance. *I'm going to buy something that isn't black with my first month's wages,* but then she wondered if she ought to go on wearing black so she would look more respectable.

To the left the hall opened onto a parlor, and she could dimly see the outlines of a heavy sofa, a bare, round table, and a spinet piano. There was a rag rug on the floor, but the room was bare and uninviting, and it appeared dusty even in this light.

A patter of high-button boots clattered on the stairs at the end of the hall, and Tim Ryan's seven-year-old twins burst into view. They skidded to a halt in front of the newcomers, gave Charlie a cursory inspection, and stared frankly at Elizabeth.

"You aren't very old," one of them said.

"I'm older than you are," Elizabeth said firmly. They looked just alike to her. The twins had bright blue eyes in heart-shaped faces. Their dark hair, which had been put into braids at some time during the day, curled in fine tangles about their faces. Their gray pinafores were stained with nameless substances, and the gingham dresses under them did not look much better. Their muddy black boots were scuffed on the toes.

"I told you two to change your clothes," Tim Ryan said.

"We did," one of the urchins assured him. She looked at Charlie. "How old are you?"

"Nine," Charlie said loftily.

"We're seven," the girl said. "And we have two ponies. You can ride one."

"Can I?" In Charlie's eyes, that made up for being only seven, and girls.

"This is Carrie," Ryan said, catching one of his offspring by the hand. "And this is Susannah. Now make a curtsy to Mrs. Bradley the way I showed you."

The girls made a sketchy ducking motion. Susannah said, "Can we eat dinner?"

"Well, now, I guess Mrs. Bradley can see why we need her," Tim said with exasperation and affection. "I said you could stay up and eat with us if you were good, but I don't think I'll ask if you were. Mrs. Bradley, I expect you and Charlie are hungry."

He led the way through double doors that opened to the right opposite the parlor. A massive oak table dominated the room. It was set with real china and sketchily polished silver flatware. The pine floor was in need of buffing and was overlaid with a dusty rag rug. At one end of the room was a fireplace. On the mantel was a clock that appeared to have stopped, and above it was the stuffed head of a bighorn sheep, which viewed them reproachfully as they settled at the table. John Potter joined them.

Elizabeth sat down, letting Tim Ryan hold her chair for her, and inspected Carrie and Susannah. They each had a spoon in one hand and a fork in the other, prepared for whatever might be served.

"There is nothing to eat yet," Elizabeth said gently, deciding that she might as well begin teaching table manners. "And you aren't supposed to pick up your fork until the hostess—which is me tonight—has done so."

"Oh." They laid their silverware down. "Why?"

"Because it is better to look as if you aren't hungry than to look as if you're greedy."

"Why?" one of them—Elizabeth thought it was Susannah—wanted to know.

She had better learn to tell them apart fast, she thought, or they would get away with murder. "Because being greedy is bad manners, and manners are the way we signal our good intentions to other people—like always mounting your pony from the side he's used to, or giving presents to the other side at a treaty meeting. It makes the other person comfortable, and they know that you mean to be friends."

Susannah appeared to be mulling this over, and Tim Ryan gave Elizabeth a look of slightly surprised approval.

"What if you don't want to be friends?" Carrie inquired.

"You do it anyway, at least till you're grown," Ryan said. "By then it's supposed to have sunk in. Here's dinner."

Elizabeth turned her head as the smell of hot food filled the room. The largest woman she had ever seen set a cast-iron pot on a trivet with a thud in the middle of the table. The woman had dark copper-colored skin and two long black braids, wrapped in leather thongs. She wore a shapeless, red-checked Mother Hubbard, which gave her mountainous form the appearance of a Turkish chair draped in a tablecloth. Elizabeth stared at her helplessly and then fixed accusing eyes on Tim Ryan.

The green eyes glinted back at her. "This is our cook, Little Deer," he said blandly. "Little Deer, this is Mrs. Bradley, and her son, Charlie."

"Glad to meet you," Little Deer said. "Mr. Ryan, you want biscuits?"

"Yes, please."

Little Deer left, and Elizabeth glared at Tim Ryan. "My chaperone, I presume?" She knew that most white women considered themselves better than Indians. As a chaperone Little Deer would rank on a level with Ryan's ranch hands.

"Well, all you said was a woman," Ryan said. "You didn't say anything about what color."

Elizabeth opened her mouth and closed it again as Little Deer came through the kitchen door with a plate of hot biscuits. There did not appear to be any butter.

He was just waiting to see what I'd do when I saw her,

Elizabeth thought furiously. Now she was sure she ought to take the first train back to Virginia. Rebelliously, she decided that she would be damned if she would.

She picked up the ladle that stood in the iron pot and began to dish out whatever it was onto the children's plates. "Mr. Ryan, if you will pass me your plate, please, I'll be glad to serve you," she said with pointed politeness.

Though Ryan ate his dinner with no further remarks, John Potter made conversation with the new housekeeper as he hungrily ate his meal. He did not think Ryan was going to get the best of her. After all, she had stood up to the shock of seeing Little Deer. Maybe she could teach the blasted woman to cook something besides buffalo stew. John strongly suspected that there was prairie dog in this one, but he thought he had better not say so.

After they had eaten the stew and the butterless biscuits, Little Deer produced a pie for dessert that, Ryan informed Elizabeth, was vinegar bean. It was not as bad as she had expected, but she suspected that it was the only dessert Little Deer knew how to make.

When they had finished, Ryan kissed the girls goodnight, reminding them to brush their teeth. He told Elizabeth that her room was just behind the parlor and that there was one next to it for Charlie. He then disappeared upstairs behind the girls. John Potter tipped his hat and vanished through the front door. A stunned Elizabeth was left standing in the hall with Charlie.

Her room proved to be a narrow chamber with a white iron bedstead, a cherry dresser with a mirror over it, and an oak wardrobe. Someone had apparently given the room a recent scrubbing in her honor; it was certainly cleaner than the rest of the house.

While Charlie bounced on the bed, she unpacked her trunk, which John Potter had left at the foot of the bed. The trunk contained all that she owned in the world. Mattie had warned her to take only serviceable gowns and leave her silks at home, and that had made them both giggle: Elizabeth had only serviceable gowns. She had brought the only remnant of her girlhood, a rose silk ball gown. Now out of style, it was meant to be worn over hoops, but there were twenty yards of material in it, and it could be made over. The rest of the trunk was taken up with things Mattie had warned her would be hard to come by in the West—her Bible, a dictionary, a few novels and volumes of poetry, and women's magazines. There was also a slat bonnet, a few family photographs, her father's sword, and as many of Charlie's toys as could be jammed into the remaining space.

"Do I have to go to school tomorrow?" Charlie asked, watching her sort their meager possessions.

"School? I hadn't even thought—no, tomorrow's Friday. We'll take tomorrow and the weekend to get settled in. You can start school on Monday." She had a feeling that if she wanted the girls in school tomorrow she would have to escort them.

She handed Charlie a nightshirt. "Go find the privy and then get into bed. No, come and tell me where it is first." There were chamber pots under the bed, but Elizabeth suspected that she would be the person to empty them.

When Charlie was settled in his own room, a smaller and simpler version of her own, Elizabeth took a candle and made her way to the privy in her nightgown and woolen wrapper. Then, crawling into bed, she blew out the lamp and wondered what had been in Mattie Ferris's mind when she had sent her out here.

Elizabeth decided that Mattie thought her brother needed a wife, not a housekeeper, so she sent him one. Evidently Tim Ryan did not want another wife, or he would have married by now. Elizabeth, with only Charles Bradley to go by, could think of no reason to want a husband. It had been a relief to sleep alone and know that Charles would not come in, half drunk and amorous. While always gentlemanly, Charles had not believed that women were supposed to enjoy lovemaking, so he had never given her the chance. Elizabeth knew that she could have enjoyed it, but she also knew that Charles would have been horrified if she had suggested it. So she had lain patiently while Charles did what he wanted and then had ached in frustration long after Charles had gone to sleep. She wondered if

Tim Ryan had been that kind of husband; somehow she did not think so.

Elizabeth pushed these disturbing thoughts away and mused instead about Ryan's oddly assorted household. The girls with their ragamuffin pinafores and impish faces were three-fourths devilment, but cute. John Potter seemed a pleasant, friendly soul. How Tim Ryan had come by Little Deer was a mystery. Most ranchers had a man or occasionally a white woman as cook. Elizabeth had heard that some men in the West took squaw wives, women they did not bother to marry, but Elizabeth could not begin to imagine Tim Ryan in bed with Little Deer. She might be working for cheaper wages, Elizabeth thought, but Ryan did not strike her as miserly either. After all, Elizabeth's own salary was certainly quite generous. She could not make sense of it. Whatever it was, it was not for her cooking. *I'm going to teach her to make pie crust tomorrow*, she thought sleepily. Better to dream of pie crust than Timothy Ryan.

In Shawnee, George Bigelow pushed himself back from the table in the dining room of the Sawyer House Hotel and ambled through the double doors that separated the dining room from the saloon. He rested one foot on the brass rail, leaned his elbows on the bar, and ordered a whiskey.

"Took your time," a gray-haired man beside him muttered, and Bigelow looked at him in mock surprise, as if he had just noticed him.

"I believe you must be early," Bigelow said. He had seen the man standing at the bar while he was halfway through his dinner, but he had no intention of hurrying his meal for a hired thug. "Let's sit down, why don't we?" he suggested, and the man followed him to a table. Bigelow put the whiskey bottle on it, and the other man filled his glass.

"Supposin' you fill me in," the man suggested.

"You don't need any more details," Bigelow said. "You've been out to look at the place. Are you going to do it or not?"

The man shook his head. "I like to know what I'm up against. I don't hire on blind, not for you, Bigelow, not for anyone."

"I want that squatter discouraged," Bigelow said. "That's what you do, Parker. Isn't it? Discourage people with a little kerosene and a match?"

Parker sipped his whiskey. "You got any particular reason?"

"Do I need one?" Bigelow snapped. "They're all over, fencing off range, getting in the cattlemen's hair. This squatter's smack on the edge of my land, running a herd of cows he probably stole from me!"

Parker nodded. Cattlemen always thought homesteaders were cow thieves. Probably were, some of them, and it was a good excuse for running them off the range. Parker did not care who was right, just as long as he was paid. "I ain't cheap," he said.

"I don't give a damn," Bigelow said. "I've already tried to buy the son of a bitch out, and he won't sell. I want a professional job that won't implicate me. You guarantee that, and I'll pay your fee."

"I reckon I can do that," Parker said. "He'll be happy enough to sell when I get through. Course, if you want him killed, it'll cost you more."

"I want him out," Bigelow said. "I don't waste money. You just soften him up enough to sell out. If that doesn't work, we'll talk again."

"You got it." Parker drained his glass. "Tell me about the neighbors."

"What about them?" Bigelow said, exasperated.

"Are they squatters or ranchers? Who has the next spread over? Are they with you in this, or do I gotta watch my back?"

"He's a rancher," Bigelow said in disgust, "but you gotta watch your back. Tim Ryan's got a pious soft spot for the plight of the squatter, and this one used to work for him."

"That's gonna cost you a hundred extra," Parker said. His expression indicated that his price was not negotiable.

Bigelow slammed the whiskey bottle down on the table and stood up. "Just do it," he growled.

*   *   *

An hour later, upstairs in Meg Callahan's parlor house, Bigelow began to relax. He leaned back on the crocheted coverlet and let plump little Sadie pull one of his boots off.

She was wearing a green silk wrapper with a froth of lace down the front, and her white breasts swelled enticingly over the ribbons on her corset. She winked one carefully made-up eye at him and ran her fingers up inside his trouser leg. Mr. Bigelow liked the girls to undress him. She pulled the other boot off and began to unbutton his trousers. He lay back on the bed with a satisfied grunt, and Sadie deftly unhooked her corset front with one hand while she fondled him with the other. She knew just what Mr. Bigelow liked. He was her favorite customer. He made her do most of the work, and sometimes he wanted odd things, but he always paid for them.

Sadie looked up at him and gave him a mock pout.

"One o' these days you'll go and get married, Mr. Bigelow, and then what am I gonna do for company?"

George Bigelow laughed and pulled her up onto the bed, squealing. The wrapper slid to the floor in a slither of green silk. "Wives aren't nearly as much fun as whores." He pulled her drawers down and smacked her bottom.

Sadie frowned. Meg did not like customers calling them whores. "We're 'companions,' Mr. Bigelow," she said with as much dignity as she could muster upside down.

"Of course you are." Bigelow swung her up onto his lap and tickled one breast where it peeped out of her open corset. Sadie giggled. He tugged her drawers off and dumped her onto the bed.

"Don't tell me you don't have any married customers?" he teased, guiding her hands to where he wanted them. He was beginning to breathe hard under Sadie's expert caresses.

After he had spent himself, she lay back on the rumpled pillows. She ached, unsatisfied. He had not taken long enough, but Mr. Bigelow never bothered about that. Sadie nestled against him and gave him a coy look. Maybe he would want her for all night. That would be nice.

Bigelow sat up and groped for a cigar in his discarded vest. He lit it and leaned back against the headboard of the big cherrywood bed. "You think you could find me a drink, honey?"

Sadie pulled on her wrapper. "You gonna stay?"

"Can't do that, honey. Got business to take care of."

Ten minutes later, he ambled down the stairs, refreshed, cigar in one hand and drink in the other. Viewing the clientele, he noted with some amusement that he had not been wrong when he had joked with Sadie about married customers. Most of them were single men, but there were three or four here tonight whose wives would lay them out if they knew where their husbands were.

George Bigelow had begun to consider marriage, but he did not intend to let that deprive him of Sadie's company. A respectable woman would faint if he suggested some of the things that Sadie did for him. With his social and political ambitions, Bigelow wanted a decorative hostess from a background that would open a few doors for him. If she were poor enough to be grateful for the chance to do it, all the better. He was beginning to think that he might have just met the woman. Mrs. Bradley would be a pretty armful to take to bed at night, without having to pay for it, but she definitely would not be enough. A well-trained wife ignored where her husband found his pleasures.

He paused in the crimson-carpeted parlor and nodded to Meg Callahan, who was resplendent in a bronze satin evening dress with a green heron's feather in her hair. The parlor, with its red-medallioned wallpaper and opulent decoration of shawls, fringes, fans, and draperies, was crowded with men and laughing, squealing women. The parlor table held a silver platter of sandwiches and little iced cakes. Meg Callahan's butler circulated with a tray of drinks.

Meg ran the most refined house in the territory. There were plenty of whores in Wyoming, but those at Meg's were at a premium—pretty, clean, cultured, and ladylike, attributes that Meg had instilled in them herself. They could sing the latest songs around the parlor piano, could eat a six-course dinner with the right utensils, and went to church every Sunday, to the scandal of the town ladies. Bigelow was aware that a number of her girls had made good marriages to men from other towns.

Meg's establishment was expensive. She set the best table, employed a French cook, and provided a better dinner than the one at the Sawyer House. Dinner was free if the gentlemen availed themselves of the services of her girls afterward. Otherwise, they paid restaurant prices for it. The back room at Meg's had become a private club, and there was usually a gentlemanly poker game going there, where a man could be sure he would not get either cheated or shot.

Meg had never bothered to hire a bouncer, but she did have Howler, a dog who, according to Meg, was the offspring of a prairie wolf and a farm dog. Howler was a good bodyguard.

Bigelow looked around the room as the notes of a piano punctuated the talk and laughter. A slender young man in wire-rimmed spectacles plunked away at the keyboard, while one of the girls sang softly to his accompaniment:

I dream of Jeannie with the light brown hair,
Borne, like a vapor, on the summer's air . . .

"Evening, George." One of the men gathered around the piano nodded at him. With his arm around a girl, he was singing happily off key.

"Evening, Elias." A steady customer at Meg's, Elias Hamill was a rancher who had started his spread about the same time that George Bigelow and Tim Ryan had begun theirs.

"You get that squatter squared away?" Hamill grinned.

Bigelow snapped his head around. "What do you mean?"

Hamill chuckled. "I heard some of your boys just happened to let a few cows stray through the Langs' garden patch," he said. "After they accidentally cut some fence."

"Oh," Bigelow said, relieved. "Now, you don't think I put them up to that," he added with mock piety. "They were just expressing their private opinions about homesteaders."

"Well, if you ask me, you ought to give those boys a raise," Hamill said. "They got good opinions." He gave a hoot of laughter and then, seeing that Meg Callahan was listening, dropped the subject with a sheepish look.

Bigelow looked at him sourly. He did not care what Meg thought, but Meg was known to have a soft spot for any underdog—and Hamill was known to have a soft spot for Meg.

A small, black-masked face peered out at them from under the piano stool, and Hamill bent down and fed it a watercress sandwich. George Bigelow regarded its shoe-button eyes and twitching whiskers with dislike. The raccoon emerged from under the piano stool, with the sandwich in its mouth, and sniffed at Bigelow's boots.

Meg and her damned animals, he thought. He drew his foot back.

"The last time I was here, that thing stole my watch," he informed Meg. "A whorehouse is no place for animals."

"McKinley's a resident," Meg said. She had found the raccoon when it was a youngster, caught in a trap. It had the run of the house and stole biscuits from the dinner table. The customers could put up with it or leave. "And I've told you gentlemen before: This is a 'parlor house.'"

Bigelow raised an eyebrow. "I've always believed in calling a spade a spade."

"Indeed? I had heard you preferred being called a gentleman rancher to a fence-cutting land thief."

Bigelow gave her a tight-lipped smile. Meg Callahan was getting a damned sight too uppity, even for a high-class whore. He was aware, however, of a long gray nose peering at him from around the draperies that hung at the doorway between the parlor and the dining room. That wolf, or whatever it was, had the run of the house, too.

"Now don't tell me where you get your political opinions from, Mrs. Callahan," he said. "Do let me guess— Tim Ryan, the homesteader's friend? You ought to be more careful who *your* friends are." He retrieved his broad-brimmed hat from the oak hall tree by the door, tipped it, and departed.

Bigelow stalked around to the hitching post, tactfully located at the rear of the house, and unhitched his horse. *Meg'd better watch what she says*, he thought.

Cattlemen came from all over the territory to spend time and money at Meg's. If she started spouting Tim Ryan's wrongheaded notions about letting homesteaders and cow thieves in, she could find herself with nobody but a bunch of oat-growing homesteaders with only nickels in their pockets on Saturday night. What Bigelow could not figure was why Ryan, who should be siding with the ranchers, was favoring the homesteaders as they fenced off chunks of the cattle range. Ryan said it was because the homesteaders had the law on their side, but Bigelow could not see what that had to do with it. The law was made by some jackass in Washington who had probably never been to Wyoming Territory, much less on a longhorn beef ranch.

George Bigelow glowered and swung his horse around toward town. He would wait till he got Parker's report. Then, first thing in the morning, he would tell the town's only lawyer, Robert Cummings, to make that squatter another offer. Cummings had been insisting there was no legal way to get the squatter off, and he had been too dainty fingered to do something about it for Bigelow. Now George Bigelow was doing it himself. By morning Montana Lang would be ready to take that offer.

Meg stared at the door for a long time after George Bigelow had left, a troubled frown on her face. Bigelow was a good customer; he carried a lot of weight, and Meg would not want to lose him. But if he was going to fight with Tim Ryan, Meg was not going to help him.

Meg Callahan had met Tim Ryan years before when Shawnee had been a tent city on a cow trail. She and Ryan had been bedmates long before he had gone to North Carolina and brought back a wife. Meg had known long ago, when she first fell in love with him, that Tim Ryan was a gentleman in every sense of the word—too much of a gentleman to marry a woman like Meg and too much of a gentleman ever to delude her that he might. Even so, after he had lost Caroline, Meg had let herself believe that Ryan might want her as his wife, but he did not. Now he did not even sleep with her, although he did once in a while pay one of her girls for that privilege. Sometimes at night Meg lay in bed longing for Tim Ryan.

She turned back to her customers. She did not trust

George Bigelow one inch. Nobody in his right mind would.

Parker looped his horse's reins around a cottonwood branch and cocked his head, listening. The cloudy night was black as pitch and still. From the barn a hundred yard's away, he could hear the occasional faint snort of dozing horses but nothing else. Bigelow had said there was no dog, and Bigelow had better be right. Parker could not stand dogs; they were bad for a man in his business.

He eased forward, glancing between the barn and the darkened house beyond it. As he pulled the barn door open, a horse blew down its nose at him curiously. Parker closed the door and lit a match, shielding it with his hand. The horse threw its head up, startled.

A kerosene lantern hung on a nail just inside the door, and Parker lifted it down. Good enough. He would not need the jar of kerosene he had brought in his sack. Bigelow would like that—Monty Lang would not be able to prove he had not left the lantern burning himself.

Parker lit the lantern and held it up, looking for a good spot. There was a pile of clean hay at the other end of the small barn, beyond the stalls. He grinned. Then he smashed the lantern against the wall and dropped it in the straw. Flame flickered, danced, and began to eat at the hay.

Parker got out in a hurry. By the time the flames had begun to eat at the barn walls, he was on his horse and gone, a breath of vicious wind in the darkness.

"Monty!" Emma Lang rolled over on the straw mattress and shook her husband frantically. "Monty! Wake up!" Outside in the night, a terrified whinnying rose and fell.

Monty Lang sat up in bed, trying to push away the fog of sleep.

"Monty!" Emma, at the window, shrieked and ran for her shoes and wrapper. "The barn's on fire!" Through the open shutters the screaming of the horses intensified.

Monty was out of bed, struggling into his pants and boots, grabbing the first folds of cloth he could put his

hands on. Outside, he dipped what he had grabbed—two
of his shirts and one of Emma's dresses—in the rain barrel
and raced for the barn.

Emma ran behind him, her eyes wide and horrified.

"Get back!" Monty shouted at her.

"The horses!"

"Get back!" Monty flung himself over the corral fence
and yanked the barn door open. Clouds of billowing, acrid
smoke rolled out, overwhelming him. He put one of the
wet shirts over his face and dived inside. In the barn he
was engulfed in a hellish mixture of flame and smoke too
thick to see through. The frantically plunging horses rock-
eted back and forth in their stalls as he felt his way toward
them. A flailing hoof lashed out and caught him in the
shin, and he stumbled. The horse reared over him, and
Monty rolled to one side as the terror-stricken animal
burst through the stall door. He caught at a trailing halter
rope and hung on while the animal reared and thrashed.
Choking on the smoke, he got the other wet shirt over its
eyes and nose and stumbled toward the door.

Outside, Emma stood rooted to the ground. When Monty
did not come out, she ran to the rain barrel and snatched
up the dress he had dropped beside it. Her heart thud-
ding, she was running for the barn door when Monty
stumbled through it with the horse.

"Get him out of here!" He handed her the halter rope
and snatched the wet dress from her hand. Before she
could speak, he had plunged into the barn again.

Coughing, Emma led the horse from the corral and tied
it to the hitching rail in front of the house. The horse
stood quivering, ready to bolt into the darkness. Emma
pulled the wet shirt away from its nose and tied it more
tightly around the animal's eyes. If it could not see the
fire, it would stand quietly.

Emma watched the angry red flames lick out from the
barn windows. She put her hands to her mouth. *Monty*.

The shrieking of the horse still in the barn stopped
suddenly, and a ring of flame outlined the door. Emma
ran for the rain barrel and filled the bucket that lay beside
it. She dashed back to the burning doorframe, and as she
flung the water at it, the liquid sizzled into steam, scalding

her face and hands. She stepped backward and was about to take the bucket and run back to the barrel for more when she saw her husband tear through the door with his shirt on fire. Behind him was the terrified horse, its mane already dancing with sparks, its eyes and nose covered with wet cloth. Monty hit the ground and rolled while Emma beat the sparks in the horse's mane with her bare hands. The horse, singed but unhurt, shook the wet dress from its head and crashed through the corral fence into the night.

Monty rose and stepped next to his wife, who now held the empty bucket in her hand, and together they looked hopelessly at the burning barn. The rain barrel and the pump, which was behind the house, were too far from the barn to do any good, with nothing but buckets to carry the water. The barn roof was already alight, and as they watched, a piece of it crashed down in a shower of sparks.

Monty took the bucket from Emma and set it gently on the ground. "It's gone," he said. He saw her scalded hands in the hellish light and limped to the rain barrel with the bucket. He filled it, brought it back, and stuck her hands in it.

Emma's face was covered with ashes and tears. "Can't we do anything?"

"We can watch it burn," he said wearily. "Keep it from spreadin' to the house." He turned and stalked away from her toward the corral fence and laid his head on the top rail. *Damn them*, he thought. *Goddamn them*.

After a moment, Emma took her hands out of the water. She picked up the bucket and went over to him and poured the cool water down the back of his charred shirt.

Chapter Three

Elizabeth Bradley woke at five A.M. to a furious clanging that sounded as though someone were beating a tin washtub to pieces with a shovel right outside her window. She drew the gingham curtains, opened the shutters, and peered out groggily. Little Deer, in her red-checkered Mother Hubbard, was flailing away at an iron triangle that hung from a post in the ranch yard. Shivering, Elizabeth splashed her face with cold water from the pitcher that sat in a basin on the washstand and quickly began to pull on her clothes. She wondered with a shudder if Broken R residents always got up at five.

Tim Ryan was already in the dining room, just finishing a breakfast of steak and biscuits, when she arrived.

"Grab a biscuit, Mrs. Bradley, and I'll show you around," Ryan said. "We're starting the spring branding today, and I don't have much time."

Elizabeth refused the biscuit and followed him through the kitchen. A red setter bitch got up from under the kitchen table and followed, tail waving.

"This is Frieda," Ryan said. The setter lolled her tongue in friendly fashion at Elizabeth. "She's pretty brainless," he noted with affection, "but she's a good dog." Frieda certainly did not look as if she had been overly endowed with intelligence, but she had a cheerful air about her and a beautiful copper-penny-colored coat.

Outside, Ryan's cowhands, six regular men and four

extra ones hired for the roundup and branding, were saddling their ponies and driving spare mounts into a cavvy, the traveling herd of remounts under the charge of the wrangler. Provisions supplied by Little Deer were being loaded into a Conestoga wagon.

"We'll do the nearby ranges in the next couple of days," Ryan said. "Then we'll be gone for about a week to pull in the strays." He pointed to a long, low building with smoke rising from the chimney. "That's the bunkhouse. And that's the foreman's cottage—John Potter's house—next to it."

Elizabeth peered through the damp, gray morning at the small whitewashed house, from which John Potter emerged, putting on his hat. He raised a friendly hand to her and headed for the corral.

"And that's the barn." Ryan waved a hand at a weathered building across the yard, still muddy with melting snow. "I keep Jericho and the girls' ponies in there. I'll find you a gentle one to ride if you like. The hens nest up in the loft. I'm gonna build a chicken house one of these days when I get time. Make it easier to get the eggs. Little Deer chases the girls up the ladder for them when she thinks about it."

"Then there are eggs," Elizabeth said. "Good. If you will just tell me where the milk cows are stabled." The first thing she was going to do was improve whatever Little Deer was preparing for dinner.

Ryan looked startled. "Mrs. Bradley, we don't have any milk cows. This is a beef ranch."

"Do you mean to tell me that with fifteen thousand head of cattle running loose out there, there isn't one that has any milk?" Elizabeth demanded.

Tim Ryan chuckled, his green eyes gleaming at her from under his hat brim. "Mrs. Bradley, if you want to try milking a longhorn, I'll have one of the boys rope one for you."

Elizabeth had seen the longhorns: rangy red beasts with long, curving horns, and wild, rolling eyes. "No, thank you. But those children need milk and butter, and the cooking would be better, too. A nice Jersey cow," she said firmly. "That's what we need."

"Certainly," Ryan said. "I'll just send for one by mail order."

"Mr. Ryan, there must be a milk cow somewhere in Wyoming Territory," she said, trying to sound sweetly reasonable.

Ryan looked at her. *She's going to dig in her heels until she gets her damned cow,* he thought. There she stood, looking no more than nineteen, giving him that muleheaded look, with her blonde hair curling in the mist, wearing another old black dress that was worse than the one she had worn yesterday. Suddenly, he grinned.

"All right, Mrs. Bradley, I'll see what I can do." He had just remembered that Meg Callahan kept a couple of milk cows, imported from the East at great expense, to give cream and butter for her dining room. "But it's gonna take a couple of days." First he had to convince Meg to give him the cow.

Elizabeth smiled, and her whole face glowed. "Thank you, Mr. Ryan. I think you'll be glad once you have the cow. And if there are vegetable seeds available in town, I'll see what I can do about getting a garden planted."

Ryan smiled back. If she could make peace, he guessed he could, too. "I expect it would be good for the children at that. But you're not to hoe a garden. You tell me what you want, and I'll have one of the boys dig it up for you."

"Morning, ma'am." John Potter joined them, a wagon harness over one arm. "As soon as the boys get off, I'll go pick up those supplies," he said to Ryan. "Is there anything you need, Mrs. Bradley?"

"Why don't you let me go?" Elizabeth said. She smiled at them both. "I intend to establish myself right away as a respectable, hardworking housekeeper before anyone decides anything else. And you look as if you have enough on your hands today."

"That's kind of you, ma'am," John Potter said. "Can you handle a wagon and team?"

"Can we go?" All three children materialized at her side as if they had sprung out of the ground like mushrooms.

"Yes, I think so," she said to John Potter, and then she looked at the children. "And yes to you too, if you promise to behave yourselves and go to school on Monday."

"Yes'm," the girls answered in unison.

"I'll just fetch my bonnet."

"Eat something," Ryan called after her.

In the house, Elizabeth gave the fried steak a look of disdain, but she swallowed half a cup of coffee and ate a biscuit while she put on her bonnet. When she came down the front steps again, Ryan had the harness in his hand and the Winchester rifle.

"You can take Jericho and Tillie," he said. "Can you shoot this thing?"

Elizabeth nodded, but she was startled when he handed her the harness. "You want to see if I know what I'm doing!" she said indignantly.

"Yeah." He lounged in the barn door.

Elizabeth gave him a look that she hoped conveyed what she thought of a gentleman who let a lady harness a wagon, and set about hitching up Jericho and Tillie.

"I guess you do know what you're up to," Ryan said after a minute. "Unexpected talent for a lady."

"Mr. Ryan," Elizabeth said, "men have no idea of the things ladies did during the war, while all the men were fighting the Yankees."

"No, I guess we don't at that." He took a stiff harness buckle out of her hands. "Here, I'll finish up. You go and collect those kids." The children appeared as he spoke, and Ryan heaved them up into the back of the wagon.

After Elizabeth had taken her place, he put the Winchester on the floor under her feet. "Just a precaution," he explained. "Now, no leanin' over the edge, you kids, and take turns in a well-behaved manner if you want to sit up front."

"Yes, sir!"

"Just tell Fishburn's to put the things on my account," he went on to Elizabeth, "and order anything else you think we need. I'll give you an advance on your wages if there's anything you want for yourself." He smacked Jericho on the rump. "And get yourself some calico. Something that doesn't make you look like an undertaker."

"That's very kind of you, Mr. Ryan," she said, giving him one of her dazzling smiles.

It was a two-hour drive into town. Frieda, who had

decided to accompany them, traveled the first five miles on a zigzag path, dashing off into the distance and back again, barking furiously at prairie dogs. When that palled, she lay down in the wagon track some distance ahead of them, tongue hanging out, and refused to budge.

"What do you want now, you feckless animal?" Elizabeth viewed her with exasperation.

"She's tired," Carrie volunteered. "She's gonna have puppies."

"I see. Well, she'd better ride then." She gave the reins to Charlie, who was taking his turn riding on the seat beside her, and hauled Frieda into the wagon, where she rode happily, barking at invisible foes.

"Where did you come from?" Carrie inquired suddenly.

"Virginia," Elizabeth said. "That's on the other side of the country. Charlie, it's time to let Carrie have a turn up front now." She was beginning to be able to tell the girls apart. Charlie and Carrie traded places, and he and Susannah leaned their elbows on the back of the wagon seat between Elizabeth and Carrie.

"Why did you come to Wyoming?" Carrie asked. "Pa— Papa came from North Carolina, but he didn't like it. Did you like Virginia?"

"Very much," Elizabeth said. "But it's not as nice as it used to be, and I needed a job, just like everybody else."

"I like Wyoming," Charlie announced. "I'm staying."

Charlie had also decided that Carrie and Susannah were all right. They were girls, and only seven, but they did not act like any girls he had ever known. They had promised to show him where a good fishing hole was, and take him to watch the cowhands brand calves. Better than anything, Mr. Ryan had promised him a horse.

"We're both staying, dear," Elizabeth said, understanding that Wyoming was a very exciting place to a young boy who had been growing up in a family of elderly aunts in Virginia.

"Did you have cows in Virginia?" Carrie asked.

"Only a milk cow, dear," Elizabeth said, thinking ruefully of her argument with their father on that subject.

"What happened to your husband?" Susannah asked. "Was he killed in the war?"

"No, but he was wounded, and he was never really well after that."

"Shhh!" Carrie reached back and pinched Susannah. "You're not supposed to ask things like that!"

"Oh. Is that why you didn't have any more children?" Susannah asked.

Elizabeth kept her eyes straight ahead on the road and managed not to burst out laughing at Susannah's notion of tact. They were unsettlingly knowledgeable for seven-year-olds.

"No, dear. God just didn't send me any more," she said, when she thought she could keep a straight face. "And that isn't the sort of question you ought to ask, either. When we get home again," she said quickly, before Susannah could think of something else to ask, "I want to look through your clothes and see what you have to wear to church on Sunday."

"Church?" Carrie gave her a horrified look.

"Church. And Sunday school, too. And we must look at your school clothes. If you'll behave yourselves, I'll buy you each a stick of candy at Fishburn's, as a reward in advance. That means if you take the candy, you're honor bound to be good afterward."

The girls looked at her respectfully. That was sneaky. They decided that this new housekeeper was all right, even if it meant going to school every day. They were supposed to go to school, of course, but if their father saw them ride off in the morning in the right direction, he generally did not notice if they came back again a short time later. Mrs. Bradley, they guessed, was going to notice.

Fishburn's General Store was presided over by Elvina Fishburn, who appeared businesslike in a striped apron with her gray hair skimmed back into a bun. It was a long single room with floor-to-ceiling shelves full of canned goods, tea, tobacco, tin and copper kitchenware, cloth, scrub brushes, work boots, and nearly anything else that a rancher or homesteader might want. Sacks of flour and coffee beans were pyramided beside the counter, and there were pickles in a barrel by the door. A little cage at the end of the counter housed the pigeonholes and desk where Elvina and her husband, Joe, served as postmasters for Shawnee. Under the counter, with its brass cash register, were glass-fronted bins of licorice, cinnamon drops, peppermint sticks, and lemon candy. While the children pressed their noses to the bins, trying to make up their minds, Elizabeth wistfully eyed the bolts of taffeta and faille stacked on a high shelf. She could not afford them, but remembering Tim Ryan's ungallant instructions, she thought she would buy a length of calico. There was a pretty blue one, pin-dotted with red, and some red ribbon just the right color on the ribbon spindle near the bolts.

There were three other women in the store besides the proprietress. The one being waited on at the counter was pretty, with obvious paint on her face, though she did not look well dressed enough to be employed by Meg Callahan. Elizabeth thought she might be one of the girls who danced at the Webfoot Saloon for a dime a dance. Carrie and Susannah, who seemed to know a lot of unsuitable things, had told her that the Webfoot had a piano and was the rowdy saloon, while people in the Sawyer House saloon had to behave themselves.

Since the other two women were ignoring the young woman at the counter, Elizabeth tactfully did so, too. When the woman had gone, one of the other customers, who looked like a homesteader's wife, with a sunbonnet and a faded calico dress with men's work boots sticking out from under it, gave the closing door a look of disgust.

"You hadn't ought to serve women like that, Elvina Fishburn!"

"When business is so good I can afford to turn down some of it, I'll think it over," Elvina said placidly. "What can I do for you, Amabel?"

"Sack of sugar, and some chewin' tobacco for Seth," Amabel said. "And a bottle o' bluing." She took a crumpled bill from a coin purse and put it on the counter.

When Elvina Fishburn had tied up the bluing and the tobacco into a neat parcel with newspaper and string, the homesteader's wife tucked it under her arm and slung the sugar over one shoulder. Noticing the children standing by the candy bins, she turned to survey the newcomer with a stern gaze. "You must be Ryan's new housekeeper," she announced. "You're mighty young." She stumped out with a nod to the other patiently waiting customer. "Mornin', Miz Cummings."

Elizabeth looked after her helplessly and saw that Mrs. Cummings was trying not to giggle. She had a curling fringe of red-gold hair under a fashionable hat and gray eyes in an almost-pretty face. She held out a hand to Elizabeth.

"I'm Lily Cummings," she said. "And you must be Mrs. Bradley. My husband and I are old friends of Tim Ryan's. You mustn't mind Amabel Hawks. She talks like that to everyone."

"Yes, I am Elizabeth Bradley," Elizabeth said. "And how nice of you not to say I look too young. I haven't heard anything else since I got here."

"It'll wear off when people get used to you," Lily said. "We haven't got much to talk about out here, so we always gossip about newcomers." She wondered, as Tim Ryan had, why his sister Mattie had sent someone so obviously too young.

"How are you getting along with the girls?" Lily lowered her voice a little. "They can be utter hellions, but they're sweet. It comes of not having their mother."

"They're dear," Elizabeth said, smiling at Lily Cummings.

Heavens, Lily thought, *she lights up the room. But, oh dear, she looks like Caroline.*

"I'm so glad to meet you," Lily said aloud. "We're all starved for female companionship out here. I'll come to call soon, and you must have tea with me." She gave her a conspiratorial smile. "I'll tell you about all the eligible men in town. Oh, dear, that's probably a dreadful thing to say to a widow, but there are so few unmarried women out here, respectable ones, I mean, that they're at a premium."

"I hadn't intended—I mean I hadn't thought of—"

"You may not have intended," Lily said, "but you're going to be courted anyway. Even old Mrs. Stebbins married again, and she's sixty if she's a day. Now, you must have a load of things to get if you've brought the wagon, so you go ahead. I only want some embroidery floss, and I'm still choosing colors."

"It's all ready, Mrs. Bradley," Elvina Fishburn said in a friendly voice, taking her cue from Lily. "Mr. Ryan ordered it yesterday."

"Thank you. And I'll have ten yards of that pin-dot blue calico, please, Mrs. Fishburn, and ten yards of the dark rose ribbon. I want some vegetable seeds, too. Mr. Ryan told me it was all right to put all this on his account."

"Of course," Elvina said.

"I'm going to have a new dress if it kills me," Elizabeth said to Lily, "and he's been kind enough to advance my wages." She wanted to be sure no one thought that Tim Ryan was buying her dresses. "I've been in mourning for several years, and I don't think I can stand it any longer."

"Do you have patterns?" Lily asked. "What we can get out here isn't exactly the latest thing."

"No, but I did bring the newest *Godey's Lady's Book* and *Harper's*," Elizabeth said.

Lily's gray eyes lit up with longing. "Oh, how heavenly. Will you let me look at them?"

"Of course," Elizabeth said. She felt as if she had found a friend, and that was immensely comforting.

"I shall come to call immediately," Lily said, laughing. "And your social success is assured—once they find out you have those books, there won't be a woman in town who won't call on you."

"I expect they will at that," Elvina Fishburn said with a grin. "Ought to start a whole spurt of dressmaking going. Good for business, so the candy's on the house." She looked over the counter at the children. "What do you young 'uns want?"

"I can recommend the cinnamon drops," a cheerful masculine voice said. George Bigelow stood beaming down at Elizabeth, hat in hand. "I'm delighted to see you again, Mrs. Bradley. I thought we might meet here—everyone eventually does at Fishburn's. Good morning, Mrs. Cummings, Mrs. Fishburn."

"Mornin', Mr. Bigelow. I'll just get Joe to load the wagon for Mrs. Bradley and I'll be right with you."

"No hurry," Bigelow said pleasantly.

"Good morning," Elizabeth said. "As you can see by the wagon, I am already hard at work." She tried to look like a proper housekeeper and not someone who had been gossiping about clothes with Lily Cummings.

"Commendably industrious," Bigelow said.

"Good morning, Mr. Bigelow," Lily Cummings said in a pleasant, but slightly cool voice.

"Tell me, Mrs. Cummings, has your husband had any success with that piece of land he's been negotiating on my behalf?"

"I'm afraid I don't know," Lily said sweetly. "I never meddle in Robert's business."

Elizabeth eyed her suspiciously. Lily Cummings looked like the sort of woman who would know exactly how her husband's business was progressing. *Cummings*. She remembered the name from the gilt letters on the law office door. Robert must be the lawyer.

"Ah, well," Bigelow was saying. "Much better that these things should be left to the men."

"My late husband used to say that," Elizabeth said loftily. "That has, I am afraid, something to do with the fact that we are penniless now."

"In your case, Mrs. Bradley, I am sure that any man would make an exception," George Bigelow said gallantly. "I do hope that I shall see you at church on Sunday? There are two, but the Baptist church is only a tent at the moment. St. Peter's Church of the Prairie is far more comfortable."

"Certainly," Lily said. "Do sit with us, Mrs. Bradley, and I will introduce you to everyone."

"That's very kind of you," Elizabeth said. She thought that George Bigelow had been about to invite her to sit with him. He tipped his hat again and retired, thwarted. Apparently he had decided not to buy anything after all.

Susannah, having decided on peppermint sticks, turned to watch him go. "Papa says he's a son of a bitch," she announced thoughtfully.

"*Susannah!*" Elizabeth and Lily cried simultaneously.

"*Where* did you hear such language?" Lily said. She looked at Elizabeth. "Although I suppose there's no point in asking that. She told us where she heard it. Susannah, you must not repeat the things your papa says."

"Why?"

"Gentlemen are allowed more, uh, expression in their speech than ladies, that's why," Lily said.

It occurred to Elizabeth, however, that Lily had not said that George Bigelow was *not* a son of a bitch.

"Dinner's on the table, Mr. Ryan." Elizabeth dusted her hands on her apron and hung it on a peg by the kitchen door. Tim Ryan, the children, John Potter, and what seemed like a roomful of cowboys, invited to dinner to meet the new housekeeper, trooped up the back steps from the yard, where they had been washing their hands under the pump. The cowhands all kept their hats on as usual, but tipped them politely as they passed her in the doorway. Elizabeth gave the children a quick inspection, decided they were presentable, and joined them at the table.

"You want to say grace, Mrs. Bradley?" Ryan said blandly, and the three cowboys who had picked up their forks put them down again.

"Lord, we thank Thee for this food," Elizabeth said, praying silently that it would be edible. "Make us mindful that it comes from Thee, as do all our blessings. Amen."

Elizabeth surveyed the table dubiously. She had suggested to Little Deer that she, Elizabeth, make the biscuits and the pie. Little Deer had seemed perfectly happy to let her, although she was less enthusiastic when it was clear Elizabeth expected her to watch and learn how it was done. The prairie chickens she had left to Little Deer, having been informed by Lily Cummings that the best recipe for a prairie chicken was to stew it with a rock until the rock was tender.

Tim Ryan attacked the meal with gusto, and Elizabeth felt smug until she realized that he could have been eating shoe leather for all the attention he was paying to it. As soon as he allayed his apparent starvation, he turned to John Potter.

"I want four or five hands—whatever we can spare—to

go to Monty Lang's place tomorrow morning to clear the mess and help him get a barn framed up," he said. "And bring along a spare horse. The one that took off last night came back lame."

"Gonna put us behind with the branding," John Potter commented.

"I don't give a damn," Ryan said. He looked around at the silent ring of cowboys. "And if anyone knows anything about this, speak up. Privately, if you want, but you speak up."

"Coulda been an accident," a grizzled, bowlegged man named Pony Simkins murmured.

"Like hell," Ryan said. "Monty's got enough brains to blow out a lantern." He saw Elizabeth looking at him curiously. "Pardon my language," he muttered. He then gave her a brief description of the barn burning. Elizabeth was aghast.

"Don't think I don't know who was behind it," he continued, "because I damn well—I sure do, but I doubt he lit the match himself." He looked around the table. "If I ever find out that any man of mine is involved in something like this, he's fired. Homesteaders have the law on their side whether we agree with it or not, and a man who won't obey the law will not work on the Broken R."

No one answered.

"All right, that's enough about it," Ryan said, and returned to his dinner.

Elizabeth wondered uneasily who he thought was responsible. She started to ask him, but something in his expression stopped her. She turned instead to explain to Carrie and Susannah why a lady did not dip her biscuits in the stew, even if the men at the table were doing it. She found the subject a tricky one, since she did not wish to insult Ryan's ranch hands, but the men did not seem to mind.

"You don't wanna grow up to look like me," Pony Simkins informed Susannah genially, "or you'll never get married."

If Elizabeth had her doubts about the dinner, the cowboys did not appear to. They ate everything in sight, and when dessert proved to be apple pie, they informed their boss that he had picked a fantastic housekeeper.

"You ain't gonna have trouble gettin' extra hands for the roundup if this keeps up," Simkins told him. He took another piece of pie.

There was a festive air to the dinner table now. The cowboys generally ate breakfast with the family, and dinner with them once a week on Sundays. In between, they subsisted on Pony Simkins's bunkhouse cooking. Breakfast and that once-a-week dinner with pretty Mrs. Bradley would now make working for Tim Ryan something special. Mrs. Bradley, John Potter decided, watching her with a grin, would have them eating out of her hand in about a week.

For her part, Elizabeth found that she liked Tim Ryan's men. They treated her with a rough courtliness that was appealing. All except Cal Hodges.

Cal was a lean, tanned man, handsomer than most, with the same rough air that they all had, but there was something else about him, a slyness, a faint contempt underlying the compliments he paid her about the pie.

He had said nothing specific that Elizabeth could object to; she just felt uneasy with him.

Cal lounged in his chair, tipping it back on its rear legs, and looked at her under his hat brim. "Mighty fine meal," he said. "And a better-lookin' cook than the Injun, too. Ain't she, boys?"

"Sit up to the table and shut up," Pony Simkins said, "before you bust that chair."

Cal clucked his tongue. "Ain't we fine haired?"

Simkins looked across the table at him. "You've not been here but a month, Cal," he said. "Might be better to wait a bit longer before you start shifting your weight."

"Man with your reputation can't be too careful," Sam Harkness said carefully. He was a youthful, towheaded man with a cowlick that hung over one eye. "Some folks would say you ought to be right pious."

"That a cow I see under your vest, Cal?" another man chuckled.

"You watch your mouth," Cal said with venom.

"I won't have this blowing up into a fight." John Potter pointedly glared at each man at the table. "Cal's last boss says he's a cow thief; Cal says he's not. Mr. Ryan says he's to have a chance. So that's all we're going to hear about it. You boys understand?"

"Yessir." They eyed John Potter and Cal Hodges. Cal had an unpleasant glitter in his eyes.

Elizabeth got up and began to clear away the plates. Sam Harkness put his hand on hers as she took his plate.

"That was a fine dinner, ma'am," he said. He gave her a wistful smile. "I don't suppose you'd go to church with me Sunday?"

A hoot of laughter ran down the table. The cowhands were certain Sam had not seen the inside of a church since he was baptized as a baby—and that was a good seventeen years ago.

Elizabeth shook her head gently. "I have to take all the children, Sam, but I thank you. It'll be nice to see you there," she added, smiling. She reached for the next plate as Sam realized with horror that he was trapped. She would bet he would be in church Sunday just to prove that he had not simply thought of it so he could take her.

She picked up Cal Hodges's plate, and Cal put his hand on hers, too, not lightly as Sam Harkness had done, but suggestively. Elizabeth drew back with distaste.

"What's the matter, little housekeeper? Ain't I as nice as Sam?"

"That's enough!" Tim Ryan barked unexpectedly from the other end of the table.

"Sure, boss." Cal's eyes traveled from Elizabeth's flushed face down over the bodice of her dress.

Elizabeth added his plate to her stack and disappeared into the kitchen with an angry knot in her stomach. She did not want Tim Ryan to think her presence would stir up trouble among the men, but she did not know how she could take Cal's sly glances without losing her composure. Putting the plates down by the big copper dishpan, she stood with her fists clenched, shaking.

"That is a bad one," Little Deer said. "Woman hater. Maybe one day something happen to him. The spirits get him maybe."

I ought to get rid of him, Tim Ryan thought. *But I haven't got any reason to unless he causes trouble here.*

Ryan pulled off his work clothes and hung them over the back of his bedroom chair. He was beginning to think that hiring Cal Hodges had been a mistake, but he had promised to give the man a chance, and he could not go back on it. If Mrs. Bradley complained, he would get rid of Cal. She seemed to have managed him well enough, so maybe he did not bother her.

Mrs. Bradley was getting to be a nuisance, he thought, what with cows and churchgoing. Earlier that day, a few hours after she and the children had gone to town, he had ridden in, skirting around the depot and the shantytown, to pay Meg Callahan an afternoon call and cajole her out of a cow. That had been some interview, Ryan thought, grinning as he climbed into bed. Meg ought to go into the cattle business, considering the price he paid her for the cow. He knew Meg Callahan was in love with him, and he felt badly about it, but he wanted nothing to do with a woman who loved him. He had considered going upstairs with one of Meg's girls, but even that had not been appealing. Maybe he was off women entirely—not a bad thing. He rolled over in the big double bed, trying not to notice how empty it felt.

An hour later he woke with a start, a dream floating fresh in his mind. The dream woman in his arms kept shifting: first Caroline, cold and blonde and so beautiful, her body soft and maddeningly near, with a white cotton nightgown up to her chin and down to her wrists. She lay as motionless as the feather pillows under her head, while he kissed her mouth, her ears, her throat, trying to coax some passion from her. She just lay there with gritted teeth while he poured his passion into her. Then she had become Meg, her brown hair in a wild tangle over her breasts, warm, inviting, drawing him into her, wordlessly begging him to lose himself in her, to stay with her, to love her. And then unaccountably she had become Elizabeth Bradley, naked in his arms, her blue eyes open wide, fixed on his, her lips parted in a gasp, her hair like a gold wreath around her head. He had drawn her toward him, feeling the slimness of her waist, the curve of her hips, the smooth, white skin of her legs, tangled with his. The tensed muscles of her thighs—he woke suddenly to find himself shaking.

Good God. Tim passed his hand across his brow and propped himself up on his elbows in bed. If Mrs. Bradley knew how she had figured in his dreams, she would take the first train out of the territory back to Virginia.

Chapter Four

"**Y**ou all look very nice," Elizabeth said as she inspected the children. Carrie and Susannah, scrubbed and combed, were dressed in clean pinafores and bonnets, and Charlie had on his Sunday suit. "If you think you can stay clean, you can go hitch Jericho to the buggy for me." The children darted off the veranda toward the stables.

Elizabeth pulled her gloves on and yawned. It was seven in the morning. The Reverend Mr. Leslie obligingly scheduled his service for nine to give the outlying ranchers time to get to church.

"I thought you'd like to know I got you a cow, Mrs. Bradley." Elizabeth turned to find Tim Ryan dressed in a black frock coat and string tie, with a prayer book in his hand. His green eyes were wary.

"She'll be here today," he said, peering at her. "You look nice this morning," he said. "Just right for church."

Elizabeth gave him a look from under raised brows. She had not had the time to cut out the blue calico, but she had taken the black veiling off her bonnet and pinned a cluster of pale flowers onto it. "Not so much like an undertaker?"

Ryan chuckled. "Maybe the drearier you look the better, on the first morning. Give all the old hens a good impression." He gave her one more look, jerked his eyes away, and strode down the steps toward the barn. "Reckon

53

I'll ride," he said over his shoulder. "Not much room in the buggy with that passel of kids."

Elizabeth looked after him, puzzled.

"Nice of the boss to buy the little lady a cow," a voice said in her ear.

She spun around to find Cal Hodges beside her. "You'll appreciate it when there's butter and custard on the dinner table," she said, moving quickly away from him toward the barn.

Cal kept pace with her. "Yeah, I expect that's a talented cow. Comes from a high-class herd. If you ain't too dainty to milk it."

"I have no idea what you mean," Elizabeth said irritably, wishing he would go away. She thought he knew that he made her nervous and was enjoying it.

"Didn't you know?" Cal gave her an unpleasant leer. "That's Meg Callahan's cow. Old Meg and the boss, they go way back. Some nights he don't come home at all."

Elizabeth felt her ears burning, but she would not give Cal the satisfaction of watching her squirm. "That is not my business, Mr. Hodges," she said stiffly. "Nor, I might add, should you gossip about your employer."

Cal laughed. "Just thought it'd be kinda funny, watchin' the fine little lady milkin' a whorehouse cow. But maybe that don't bother you none."

Elizabeth fled into the barn, hoping that Cal would not follow her there, and glad of the children's presence. She patted Jericho's smooth red flank and climbed into the buggy.

It was not her business, she thought angrily. Tim Ryan and what he did was no business of hers.

Elizabeth kept glancing from her hymnbook to Charlie and the twins, singing beside her. The girls did not read very well yet, but they made up in enthusiasm what they lacked in knowledge. From the end of the pew, beside Susannah, Tim Ryan's baritone rang out confidently, with Sam Harkness's tenor limping along half a note behind him.

To Elizabeth's left, Lily Cummings's voice mingled with

her husband's. Robert Cummings was a pleasant, square-faced man with a shock of unruly brown hair, which obviously had been slicked down earlier in the morning but was now standing on end. Lily had blinked in mild surprise at the sight of Tim Ryan in his black frock coat; she had goggled at Sam Harkness.

"The Lord is in His holy temple; let all earth keep silence before Him."

William Leslie, a tall gray-haired man with a long, humorous face, turned to face the congregation. St. Peter's Church of the Prairie seemed unusually full this morning, and he wondered how many of them had come to get a good look at Tim Ryan's new housekeeper.

"Dearly beloved brethren, the scripture moveth us in sundry places, to acknowledge and confess our manifold sins and wickedness. . . ."

The congregation knelt, with a rustling of petticoats and a jingling of spurs, to consider their sins. Elizabeth looked around cautiously and admired the small church.

The inside of the sanctuary was pretty, if spartan, with whitewashed walls and polished wooden pews in the front. Latecomers had to make do with folding chairs and an assortment of packing crates in the rear. There were vases of bright flowers on the altar, and a single stained-glass window, depicting the risen Christ, was above it. The window had been donated by George Bigelow, the richest man in the county, who had had it shipped from the East.

When the group from the Broken R arrived, Bigelow, hat in hand, had been at the church door to greet Elizabeth. She had sensed the angry tension between him and Tim Ryan, although they greeted each other with polished civility. Then Lily had introduced Elizabeth to as many people as possible before the service began—old Dad Henry, who owned a ranch just out of town and whose first name proved to be Ezekiel, and Clyde and Agnes Sawyer, who owned the Sawyer House Hotel. Clyde was portly and prosperous looking, with a gold chain across his embroidered waistcoat. Agnes was thin and a little overdressed for church. She gave Elizabeth a sharp inspection before she said she was sure she was charmed. Angus Ogilvie, who spoke in an almost unintelligible Scots brogue,

was another rancher. Tim Ryan had also called Monty
Lang and his new wife to be introduced. Monty was a wiry
man in his late twenties, with a weatherbeaten face. He
blinked at the sight of Sam Harkness, and Sam blushed
and said that if Monty could become pious, he could, too.
Emma Lang was a slight, big-eyed child; she wore a
yellow and white calico dress with a white embroidered
collar.

"Let us pray."

The congregation stirred once again as they bowed their
heads in prayer. Elizabeth tried to concentrate on the old
words of comfort and blessing:

> O Lord, show Thy mercy upon us;
> And grant us Thy salvation.
> O God, make clean our hearts within us;
> And take not Thy Holy Spirit from us.

When the congregation had settled back into their seats,
the collection plate was passed by Robert Cummings and
Angus Ogilvie. Mr. Leslie then preached a sermon on the
ills that a lack of tolerance for others' ways could bring
about and on the necessity for not prejudging one's fellow
man. It seemed reasonably innocuous to Elizabeth, but
there was a tension that told her he was speaking directly
to some of his flock.

After the recessional had been sung, everyone filed out
into the sunlight to talk about the sermon and get a better
look at the newcomer.

Meg Callahan, shepherding her brood into a stylish
landau, thought with satisfaction that the town of Shawnee
had something to stare at besides her girls for a change.
George Bigelow and his cattlemen friends could now deplore Mr. Leslie's sermon, while all the women could
deplore Mrs. Bradley, who was far too pretty. Meg felt a
little sorry for her, but she nevertheless wished she would
go back to Virginia.

Elizabeth stole a look at Meg's landau as it rolled smartly
down the street toward town. Cal's jibes were still in her
mind. *It shouldn't make any difference to me*, she told

herself angrily. But noticing Tim Ryan looking at Meg stirred her jealousy even more.

"Isn't she something," a young woman beside her said wistfully. "I'd like to wear a dress like that, but the school board would fire me in a minute."

Elizabeth turned to find Beth Armstrong, the schoolteacher, standing beside her. "One isn't supposed to notice her, of course," Beth whispered, "but that's awfully hard." Beth was a pretty, plump girl with a cloud of dark brown hair and a sensible-looking dress.

"Cheer up, Miss Armstrong," George Bigelow said. "You've only got two months left in the school year, and then you won't have to listen to anyone."

"I hope I won't go that far," Beth said, "but I have to admit it will be a relief not to have the school board breathing down my neck. I only say this to you, Mr. Bigelow, because you aren't on the board, and you don't have any children."

"I would never tell on a lady," Bigelow said. "Contain yourself for two months, and then you can dance a jig down the main street in your shimmy if you so desire."

"I'm getting married this summer," Beth explained to Elizabeth. "After school is out. Of course, I won't be able to teach after that. Although I really don't see why," she added with a touch of resentment in her voice.

"Because lady schoolteachers aren't supposed to know anything interesting that the kiddies might find out from them," Bigelow said, and Elizabeth smiled involuntarily. "And now, Mrs. Bradley, would you care to take a Sunday stroll—just to town and back?"

She was tempted. The sun had come out of the morning fog, and the sky was a bird's-egg blue. Everything in the crisp air smelled washed and fresh.

"Mrs. Bradley has chores to attend to," Tim Ryan said curtly, appearing miraculously at her other side.

Elizabeth looked sharply at him, bristling. "Mr. Ryan, this is a day of rest, as Mr. Leslie was telling us. Furthermore, I have Sundays off."

"What about the children?"

"The children, as you can see, are playing in the churchyard. They will keep very nicely for half an hour." The green eyes scowled at her, and she glared back. She gave her arm to George Bigelow, who tucked it possessively into his. *I believe he's courting me*, she thought, feeling uncertain about it. Nevertheless she smiled sweetly at him. "Thank you, Mr. Bigelow. I should be charmed."

Lily, who was watching Tim Ryan watch George Bigelow, touched her husband's hand. "Robert, look. Oh, dear, this is going to be a dreadful mess."

"Not your business, Lily," Robert chided her.

"It certainly is!" she said indignantly. "Tim's our best friend!"

"If Mrs. Bradley got married, it would be the best thing all around. She shouldn't be out there under Tim's nose all day. His sister should be shot. Stay out of it, if you're thinking what I think you are."

"But, Robert—George Bigelow!" protested Lily. The faint sound of laughter reached them from the couple strolling leisurely toward town.

"Then you'd better find her another suitor fast," Robert said.

"I suppose so," Lily said dubiously.

If George Bigelow was courting her, Elizabeth quickly discovered that he was not the only one. Sam Harkness continued to admire her with a shy, gentle gallantry. On Monday, old Dad Henry appeared just as she had sent the children off to school on their ponies. Apparently unable to speak he silently handed her a bunch of spring wildflowers. His bony, tortoiselike face stared earnestly at her above a clean shirt and collar. Then Tim Ryan came down the porch steps to start the day's branding and clearly embarrassed Dad Henry. Elizabeth, with a strangled look at her employer, took the wildflowers and fled into the house.

Since Sunday afternoon, after her stroll with George Bigelow, Ryan had been icily polite. He had hired her to keep house, not to flirt with every man for miles around, Elizabeth thought desperately as she stuffed the wildflowers in the vase. She was sure that he would greet the appearance of another suitor with further irritation.

"He bring you flowers," Little Deer said with interest, inspecting the chickweed and dogtooth violets that drooped over the edges of the vase. "He is looking for wife."

"Well, I'm not looking for a husband," Elizabeth said briskly.

"That don't matter," Little Deer said. "They look for you."

The next evening brought yet another caller, this time Angus Ogilvie, who rode up while Elizabeth was emptying the dishpan in the grass under an elm tree.

"Good evening, Mr. Ogilvie." She looked at him hesitantly. "Were you looking for Mr. Ryan? He's in the barn."

Angus Ogilvie regarded her gravely from the back of his pinto horse. "Do you like the pipes?" he inquired. He dismounted from his pinto, unstrapping a monstrous contraption that looked like a stiff-legged octopus from the back of his saddle, and strode toward the porch.

Elizabeth followed helplessly, carrying the dishpan. On the porch, Mr. Ogilvie solemnly inflated the bag and tried the tone with experimental squawks and moans. He tucked it under his arm and looked at Elizabeth with interest. "I dinna get many chances to play for a lady."

Elizabeth peered at him in the dusk.

"It's an art," Mr. Ogilvie said, solemnly.

Tim Ryan was in the barn, brushing down a gray roan named Beau, when he heard a low, wailing burble that made the hair on the back of his neck stand up. He and Beau looked at each other in mutual astonishment as the sound began again. It appeared to have a tune to it. Ryan tossed the brush in the tack box and picked up his hat. Venturing into the yard, he saw his housekeeper, with a dishpan in her lap, sitting on the front porch of his house listening attentively to Angus Ogilvie rendering a brisk version of "Hielan' Laddie." Ryan had no idea what the tune was; he only knew it was loud.

As he listened, dumbstruck, three heads popped out of the bunkhouse window.

"It's a calf, caught in some wire," one of them said.

"Naw, it ain't. It's a cougar. You shoot it, Sam."

"It's the end of the world," Pony Simkins said. "Weepin' an' lamentations an' gnashin' of teeth." He drew his head in again. Simkins knew some of Angus Ogilvie's ranch hands. He was sure they had sent Ogilvie over to serenade Mrs. Bradley so that he would stop playing for them.

Elizabeth, who could hear nothing but the sound of the bagpipes, looked up with a start to find Mr. Ryan standing at the end of the porch. *Oh, Lord, he'll be perfectly furious,* she thought. "Hielan' Laddie" galloped to a stop, and Elizabeth smiled appreciatively at Angus Ogilvie. "That was lovely," she said. "But now I really must go and finish my chores."

"By no means," Tim Ryan said cheerfully. She saw a wicked grin on his face in the shadow of his hat. "Sit out here and enjoy the night air. That's a fine tune, Ogilvie. You play her another one." He disappeared into the house.

Elizabeth, glancing over her shoulder, saw him in the hallway, doubled up with laughter.

Mr. Ogilvie, in a mood of gentle melancholy suitable for courting, launched into "The Flowers of the Forest."

The next morning, as Ryan sat down to breakfast, he said to Elizabeth with a straight face, "I trust you enjoyed the concert." A faint hoot of laughter and a few subdued snickers came from the cowboys at the table.

"That's a fine instrument," Sam Harkness said. "Won't be a wolf for miles around to trouble the stock. You tell him to come on back."

"Yep, flowers is nice," Pony Simkins said, reaching for a biscuit, "but you can't beat a bagpipe for distinctive courtin'."

"I enjoyed it very much," Elizabeth said loftily.

"It was awful," Charlie muttered.

"Eat your breakfast." Elizabeth swept into the kitchen, trying not to see the look of unholy amusement in Tim Ryan's cat-green eyes.

*   *   *

It soon became obvious that if Tim Ryan thought that Angus Ogilvie was funny, his amusement did not extend to Elizabeth's most persistent suitor.

On Saturday evening an elegant surrey drawn by a pair of spanking black horses pulled into the yard, and the children, who had been playing on the swing under the big elm, tumbled off it to stare in awe. When the driver leaned out, however, they retreated a few steps, and their faces took on that closed look that children wear in the presence of an adult they do not like.

"Mrs. Bradley at home?" George Bigelow inquired genially.

The children looked at each other. "Yeah," Charlie said unhelpfully.

"Well, maybe you'd ask her if she would step out for a moment."

Charlie looked as if he did not want to, but just then Elizabeth came down the front steps, wiping her hands on her apron.

Bigelow tipped his hat. "Good evening." He looked at the children. "You youngsters can run along now," he suggested.

"Good evening, Mr. Bigelow," Elizabeth said. She could see Tim Ryan standing in the barn doorway behind the surrey. "Will you come in?"

"I don't think that would be appropriate," Bigelow said. "I just stopped by to ask if you would do me the honor of escorting you to church tomorrow."

Elizabeth hesitated. "I have to take the children," she ventured.

Bigelow winced elaborately and grinned at her. "For you, Mrs. Bradley, even that. Bring 'em along."

Elizabeth smiled hesitantly. She knew she should not go to church with him so soon after her arrival in Shawnee. The whole town would talk about it. She was starting to say so when she saw Ryan approach menacingly from the barn. His green eyes were furious. She thought he was going to order her into the house, and she prepared to do battle, but Ryan just stalked past her, ignoring her, ignoring Bigelow.

"My apologies," Bigelow said, with every evidence of

contrition. "I wouldn't want to put you in an embarrassing position."

"On the contrary," Elizabeth said, anger clouding her better judgment. "I should be delighted to go to church with you." She cast a seething glance toward the house. "The children and I will be ready."

Everyone within staring distance cast speculative looks at Elizabeth the next morning as she strolled with George Bigelow on the church lawn after morning prayer. Elizabeth knew she had made a mistake.

Bigelow chuckled. "Take no notice. The good folk of Shawnee have a tendency to think that anyone who isn't hard at work is up to no good."

Elizabeth sighed. "I'm afraid Mr. Ryan feels that way where I am concerned."

"A difficult position for a woman of your obvious breeding and upbringing," Bigelow commented.

"I've grown used to it," Elizabeth said. "I've had to. And no one I knew before the war is much better off now, so I really can't feel abused."

"Was it so very different for you, before the war?" Bigelow asked sympathetically.

"Oh, yes." Elizabeth smiled. "It was lovely. But nothing lasts. We must accustom ourselves to change, I expect."

"Be of good cheer, Mrs. Bradley," Bigelow said. "There are fortunes to be made in the West." He swept his arm out, across the distant green of the prairie. "Wyoming is a land of considerable opportunity."

"So I'm told," Elizabeth said. Certainly George Bigelow had made the best use of his opportunity. She sensed that Bigelow was offering himself to her as an opportunity, and she began to consider how her life could change. George Bigelow's wife would not have to milk a cow at four o'clock every morning to have butter on the table.

"And, of course, one needn't spend all one's time in Wyoming," Bigelow was saying. "Once an outfit reaches a certain size, it can be well handled by a professional manager, leaving its owner free to enjoy more civilized comforts. I expect shortly to be able to spend nine months of the year in the East."

Opera, Elizabeth thought. *Balls, dancing, theater* . . .

"Unlike your employer," he added, "who will probably spend the rest of his life punching cows for a lack of vision."

That snapped her out of her fantasy. "Tell me, Mr. Bigelow. Why do you and Mr. Ryan dislike each other?"

"I don't suppose you could bring yourself to call me George?" he said.

"No," Elizabeth said. "Not yet."

Bigelow sighed. "Very well, I shall endeavor to be patient." He linked his arm through hers. "Tim Ryan lacks vision. I believe I mentioned that? He can't see the forest for the trees. And if he isn't careful, pretty soon he won't be able to see his cows for the squatters. Cattlemen opened up Wyoming, Mrs. Bradley. Due to the ignorance of certain fools in Washington, a cattleman can't claim more than a certain amount of land, but he can, and has from the first days here, graze his stock on the public range. We need that range, and it's always been available. If it weren't for the cattlemen, it wouldn't be clear of Indians and safe for white men. We did the dirty work. Now that we've done it, the squatters have moved in, plowing up the grass and fencing land so the cattle can't get to water. They even help themselves to our cattle. Show me a squatter, and I'll show you a cow thief."

"Surely not all of them?" Elizabeth said, thinking of Monty Lang.

"Nine-tenths of them. It's been proven over and over. If something isn't done, they'll be the end of us. Since the government, in its foolishness, has given the northern range to the Indians, this is all we've got, and by God, we're going to hang onto it. Tim Ryan supports the squatters. He's turned his back on his own kind; that's what it amounts to."

"He says the homesteaders have the law on their side," Elizabeth said. "Surely one must work within the law?"

"As I recall," Bigelow said, "the Union also felt that it had the law on its side. I don't recall that the Confederacy sat still and took the Union's word for it."

"We also felt we had the law on our side!" Elizabeth said indignantly.

"Exactly," Bigelow said. "It's all in how one views the law."

"Then perhaps the cattlemen and the homesteaders should take a lesson from that, and learn to coexist," Elizabeth said, amused in spite of herself. "It might save a certain amount of unpleasantness."

"You may pray for that day, Mrs. Bradley," George Bigelow assured her. "In the meantime, the cattlemen are going to defend themselves."

They turned at the end of the lawn to stroll again toward the church. "Do you know, I'm quite enjoying this conversation," Bigelow said. "It isn't often that one meets a woman of such principle and intelligence. Or," he added gravely, "a woman with such beautiful eyes."

Elizabeth gave up the thorny problem of the cattlemen versus the homesteaders and let him buy the children ice cream at the Sawyer House.

"And the worst of it is," Elizabeth said to Lily Cummings later, "I'm so ignorant about things out here. I don't know which of them is right."

"Neither of 'em," Robert Cummings said promptly. "Some of the small ranchers are rounding up strays, which, I might add, is how Tim Ryan and George Bigelow got their start, years ago in Texas during the war. That was, and still is, considered fair. But some of 'em are also stealing calves from branded cows, and the cattlemen have got a right to be angry about that. Nevertheless, George Bigelow has no right to try and push the homesteaders out. He's been trying to buy Monty Lang's land, or figure out a legal way to steal it from him, for months. Now he's inciting the big ranchers because he hasn't had any luck with Monty."

"Oh, dear," Elizabeth sighed.

"How interested are you in George Bigelow?" Lily said.

"Have another piece of pie, Elizabeth," Robert interrupted. "Don't let Lily mind your business for you."

"Robert thinks I'm a busybody," Lily said rebelliously, cutting the pie. "But I only asked, because if you are reaching an understanding with George, you ought to know the other reason he doesn't get along with Tim."

"Lily—" Robert said in warning.

"I think she needs to know about Little Deer," Lily said quickly. Some unspoken message seemed to pass between them.

"Little Deer—oh. Well, maybe so." Robert relaxed and gave Lily a faint grin. "I'll let you tell it, my darling," he murmured, "since you have such a flair for drama."

Lily gave him a rueful look. "It's hardly funny," she said reprovingly. "Poor thing." She turned to Elizabeth. "Little Deer is a constant reminder to Tim of something abominable George did many years ago," Lily said.

Elizabeth blinked. If she could not imagine Tim Ryan romantically linked with the mountainous Little Deer, George Bigelow was an even unlikelier prospect. "Heavens," she murmured.

Lily giggled. "It's not what you think. At least, not really." She put the pie knife down and poured fresh tea in Elizabeth's cup. "When Wyoming was first settled, there were hardly any women at all. I got to Shawnee and discovered that I was the only white woman in a fifty-mile radius. A lot of the men had squaw wives, men being what they are. When things got a little tamer, white women began to come. I'm afraid the rest doesn't make me very proud. The white women refused to associate with the men who had Indian wives. They built a nice respectable little society in Shawnee and excluded the squaw men from it. So the men started to send their Indian wives, to whom they weren't really married, back to their tribes. Because they were rejected by their white husbands and sent home, the squaw wives were disgraced in the Indians' eyes and were treated badly by the tribes. Most of them had a very unhappy time of it."

"Oh, poor things," Elizabeth said. "How dreadful."

"I feel rather uncomfortable telling you this," Lily said, "because I think George is courting you, but George Bigelow had an Indian wife, and he abandoned her in the most callous fashion."

"Not Little Deer!"

"No," Lily said. "George's Indian woman is dead. He

sent her home to her people, and she killed herself before she got there. Tim Ryan found her body on the trail. He went looking for George Bigelow and nearly killed him. I think he would have if Robert hadn't got them apart."

Sickened, Elizabeth leaned back in her chair and closed her eyes for a moment. Maybe Bigelow had not known what would happen, she thought. Or perhaps he had not cared. "And Little Deer?" she asked faintly.

"Little Deer was another squaw wife. Tim had become a friend of the chief of her tribe. Tim took Little Deer in to be his cook when her white husband sent her away. I think Chief Black Wolf was grateful to Tim for probably saving her life. Tim understands the Indians and, I think, even likes them in a way. Later that year, Little Deer's white husband was killed by Indians. We never knew if there was any connection. Life can be brutal here."

Elizabeth stood up, obviously shaken.

"I'm sorry if I've upset you," Lily said.

"No, I'm glad you told me," Elizabeth said. "I need to understand, if I'm going to live here."

Lily took her hand. "That's the biggest hurdle, dear, being willing to understand that the West isn't like anywhere else. If you can do that, you'll make it."

The thought of George Bigelow's Indian woman haunted Elizabeth as she climbed into the wagon with the children and whistled for Frieda, who was now big with pups. Maybe there was another side to the story. Perhaps Bigelow had not known what would happen. She could not ask him about it, not yet. *I'll just have to wait,* she thought, shaking out the reins.

Tillie and Jericho clip-clopped down the main street of Shawnee and out into the open land. As Susannah, Carrie, Charlie, and the dog all tried to snuggle against her at once, Elizabeth realized that she had learned one thing— the irascible Mr. Timothy Ryan had a kind heart.

Chapter Five

The next morning Tim Ryan, John Potter, and all the cowhands except Sam Harkness prepared to leave to finish the roundup and branding. Sam was staying behind to look after the Broken R and its occupants.

The cowhands loaded branding equipment into one Conestoga wagon and provisions for Pony Simkins, the bunkhouse cook, into another.

"Now don't worry, Mrs. Bradley," Ryan told Elizabeth. "You just keep the rifle handy. If there's trouble, you fire three shots in quick succession, then another three. That's a signal out here that there's trouble. Anyone who hears it will come in a hurry. Sam will have a good idea where to find us if you need me. Fine, you're all set then." He kissed the girls, hugged Charlie, who looked after him wistfully, and strode toward his horse.

"I shall endeavor not to collapse in your absence," Elizabeth muttered to his retreating back.

"When I'm bigger," Charlie announced, "I am going on a roundup."

"Right now you're going to school," Elizabeth said.

The three children groaned.

"It won't be long till school is out," Elizabeth said. "You can stand it for a few weeks more."

She watched the cowboys saddle up. They would be gone for a week, and she intended to make good use of the time. She had borrowed two bound Swedish sisters—

indentured servants, working off their passage to America—
from Lily and Agnes Sawyer, and she planned to clean the
bunkhouse thoroughly and then shake out the ranch house.

Once the men had left, Elizabeth and the women started
on the bunkhouse. They dragged all the furniture into the
yard, scrubbed it vigorously, and painted it with alum and
boiling water for the bedbugs. Then they boiled all the
clothes and bedding.

Sam Harkness, given a change of clean clothing, was
told firmly to hand over what he was wearing for the same
treatment. The young Swedish sisters giggled behind their
hands. Sam did not mind. One of them had the prettiest
hair and eyes. Maybe he could get her to teach him
Swedish, he thought. Sam really did not want to learn
Swedish, but the idea of long lessons, sitting out under a
tree somewhere with her, appealed to him.

When the bunkhouse was spotless and freshly whitewashed, they tackled John Potter's cottage.

As soon as the children left for school the next day,
Elizabeth and the sisters started on the ranch house. They
went through the girls' room first, throwing out trash but
carefully preserving treasures—pictures cut from magazines, prettily striped rocks, and a box of dead beetles.
Rugs were beaten, floors polished, bedding washed, and
mousetraps set. The bound sisters had to leave early, but
Little Deer helped cheerfully.

Elizabeth now thought of Little Deer with interest and
sympathy. She had been some man's wife, in effect if not
in name, with a house of her own, but had suddenly been
turned out because she was Indian. Elizabeth had never
thought about the Indians before, except as a vague, distant menace. Through Little Deer they became real for
her, people with pride, feelings, and ways of doing things
as mysterious to Elizabeth as her own ways must be to
them.

She smiled at Little Deer, huffing up the steps with an
armload of clean sheets. "Mr. Ryan won't know this place
when he gets back. I couldn't have done it without you."

Little Deer beamed. "Mr. Ryan is a good man: I know
that a long time."

Except for the attic, Elizabeth had saved Tim Ryan's

room till last, uneasy about venturing into his private domain. Sternly telling herself not to be ridiculous, she finally marched in with Little Deer and surveyed it. There was a blue rag rug on the floor, a tarnished brass bed, and a marble-topped dresser that must have cost a fortune to ship to the territory. Furniture he had bought for his wife, Elizabeth concluded. Curious in spite of herself, she looked for a picture of Caroline Ryan, but she found none. There were photographs of the girls, though, and two small cross-stitch samplers, marked with the prints of dirty fingers, that read "Home Sweet Home" and "Bless This House."

"They make him those for Christmas," Little Deer said. "Up in the attic, there is one their mother make—very beautiful."

There was nothing of Caroline in this room except the unpolished, dusty furniture. Mr. Ryan seemed to be a man who kept memories to himself.

"What was she like?" she asked Little Deer.

"Mrs. Ryan?" Little Deer shrugged. "I come to work for Mr. Ryan after she die. John Potter, too. We never see her. She was beautiful, that is what people say. Yellow hair like yours. But I never see a picture of her."

"No matter," Elizabeth said briskly. She began, almost defiantly, stripping the sheets from Tim Ryan's bed. His wife, his bed, his private life had nothing to do with her.

She had saved the only job that she considered fun for last—the attic. Elizabeth loved attics. They were a treasure trove of memories and history. Maybe in the attic she would find a clue to Tim Ryan. Since she had told him she was going to clean it and he had not objected, she felt she could legitimately pry.

There was a trunk of baby clothes, two of everything, lovely, delicate, carefully packed away. Caroline Ryan must have spent hours stitching them.

There were two parlor lamps with china bases and shades, painted with roses. Elizabeth seized on them with delight. She found aspic molds, fancy cake pans, and tiny cookie cutters shaped like hearts and half moons, which Elizabeth added to her pile of treasures.

In another box were sewing needles, a gold thimble, and embroidery hoops. Wrapped in tissue paper was Caroline Ryan's embroidery work: a picture of the ranch, embellished with a border of azaleas and roses that must have been a wistful memory of her life in the East. In front of the ranch house was a white picket fence and a smooth green lawn that could never have existed. Elizabeth packed all these things away again. She had her own sewing kit; it would not be right to use Caroline's. She did keep one thing from the bottom of the box—a goffering iron used to press delicate pleated ruffles into pinafores and cuffs. The goffering iron she would use.

When the house was clean from top to bottom, Elizabeth took one more step, which she knew might or might not please Mr. Ryan. She had the spinet piano in the parlor tuned. She was sure it had not been played since Caroline had died, and it would be good to have music in the house.

Surveying the piano, polished, oiled, and musical once more, Elizabeth giggled, and she saw Little Deer's mouth twitch, too. If Mr. Ryan knew what they had gone through! She had asked Lily Cummings if she knew anyone in Shawnee who tuned pianos. She had learned that the only man in town was the piano player at Meg Callahan's parlor house.

"He tunes all the pianos in town," Lily said. "Even the church's. Of course, no respectable woman can talk to him, so the men arrange it. The Sunday after the church's piano is tuned, we all pretend we don't know why, but tell each other how lovely it sounds."

"I see," Elizabeth said. She smiled sweetly at Lily's husband. "Dear Robert—"

So Robert Cummings had gone to Meg Callahan's, with stern admonitions from Lily not to look at anybody, and negotiated with the piano tuner. Then Robert had gallantly brought him to the Broken R while Elizabeth was shopping in town and having tea with Lily. Elizabeth had returned to find the piano tuned and Little Deer plunking delightedly at the keys. She knew Little Deer did not

understand why Mrs. Bradley could not talk to a piano
tuner from a parlor house, but Little Deer thought it was
funny anyway.

The spring roundup was a cooperative venture among
the ranchers, since all the cattle ranged freely. Each ranch
oversaw the roundup on its own land, accompanied by
representatives of the other spreads. Each morning they
would split into separate groups to scour the hills and
canyons where cattle might be hiding. They would re-
group in the evening to meet the chuckwagons at a prear-
ranged point, driving before them the cattle they had
gathered. At the chuckwagons, the cattle would be sorted
and the calves branded according to the brand carried by
their mothers.

By the end of the week, the roundup crews were working the foothills north of George Bigelow's Double X,
having come nearly full circle from their starting place on
the Broken R.

In a shaded ravine not far from Bigelow's ranch, three
men crouched as they prepared to brand a calf. The oldest
man, Tom Wall, flipped the calf expertly onto its side and
pinned it as he nervously glanced over his shoulder.

"Come on with that iron," he snapped, as his son Jem
pulled the branding iron from the coals. Just behind them,
the calf's mother hovered. She too was freshly branded,
the Double X on her flank turned into four diamonds.
Tom knew she would stay near while they still had her
calf. "Hustle," he snapped again. "I don't like this. We're
workin' too close to the roundup."

"Ain't gonna find loose cows no place else," Jem said.
"They got all the rest bunched up for the trail drive."

"We oughta have waited," Frank Wall said nervously.

"Waited for what?" Jem said to his brother. "To starve
to death? Without some money, we'll have to pack up."
He laid the iron, a plain two-foot rod with only a straight
bar at the tip, along the calf's flank, duplicating the qua-
druple diamond pattern he had executed on its mother.
The calf bellowed piercingly, drowning out a sound that
should have sent the three cattle thieves running.

A shot splattered the dirt by Tom Wall's foot, and he flung himself off the calf, too late to reach for his gun. Six cowboys loomed over him, their own guns leveled.

"What the hell do you think you're doing?" one of them yelled.

"You know damn well what we're doing," Tom Wall spat. He slumped. "Jesus, mister, we ain't got any food in the house. Cattle ruined what crops we could plant. My wife died last spring, and we didn't even have the money for a coffin. You tell me what else we could do!"

The cowboy shook his head. "Don't make no difference now. You ain't gonna need a coffin either." He untied his lariat from the saddle.

"Mister, no! Please!"

"You sure we oughta?" one of the cowboys said hesitantly.

The crew leader looked at him. "You're one of Elias Hamill's men, ain't you?"

The other cowboy nodded. "I just signed on."

"Then your boss would tell you the same thing," the crew leader said. He was one of George Bigelow's men, and he knew without asking what his boss would say. "Tie 'em up," he said, and the others dismounted. "If we don't take care of this, there won't be a cow safe from thieving anywhere for miles. Stock stealing's a hanging offense; always has been, with good reason."

"I still don't like it," Hamill's man said dubiously.

"You don't have to like it," the crew leader said. "You just got to do it."

Tim Ryan was in no better mood than the rest of the men on the roundup crews, all of whom were dirty, bone tired, and short tempered by now. To add to his poor disposition, he had found two calves running with Broken R cows and sporting two different, unknown brands—stolen calves that had slipped away from whatever herd they were being driven with and found their way to their mothers. If two had done that, Ryan would bet there were forty more that had not. *George Bigelow was right about range theft, damn him,* Ryan thought. *Damn and blast the men who have stolen calves and given every honest small rancher a bad name!*

He shifted wearily in the saddle. It was late afternoon, Beau had thrown a shoe, and by the time he got back to camp, dinner would be stone cold. He had sent his crew ahead with the cows, and was plodding carefully along at a walk, feeling surly, when he heard the angry shouting over a rise to the north, in the scrubby hills that the Double X men and Elias Hamill's representative had staked out for the day.

Ryan eased Beau quietly up the slope and drew rein in a clump of trees. Below him, three men were kneeling beside an open fire, their hands tied behind their backs. They were surrounded by half a dozen furious cowboys. Ryan's mouth twisted, and he kicked Beau down the hill. A freshly branded calf, just released, was squealing its indignation to an anxiously lowing longhorn cow. The branding iron lying beside the fire told of the trouble.

"What are you doing?" Ryan said, but he knew.

"You're just in time to help hang three thieving squatters, Ryan," Bigelow's crew leader said.

Ryan did not need to ask if they had proof. That running iron, its plain tip designed for altering brands, was proof enough. On the open range, where a man's brand on his cows was his only defense against theft, the mere possession of a running iron established guilt irrefutably.

"We aren't the law," Ryan said. He looked at the noose that Bigelow's crew leader was fashioning from his lariat. "That's Hank Purchase's job."

"It's our job," the crew leader said. "Now. Out here. Before some fancy-pants lawyer starts pleadin' special circumstances and gets 'em off, and every squatter in the territory starts figuring cow thieving's worth the risk."

"I swear to God we only took these two," Tom Wall said.

"Horseshit," Bigelow's crew leader said. "If you only wanted one cow to eat, you'd have slaughtered it and not messed around with a running iron."

"We tried to make it out here," Jem said. He looked to be about twenty-five, his face already lined from the struggle against the land. "Every time we'd plant, the damned cattle would come through."

"Then you been planting in the wrong place," the crew leader said. "It don't matter now."

"Hang 'em!" someone shouted, and the others joined in.

"We aren't the law," Ryan said again. "Take 'em to town. If they're guilty, they'll hang." He knew they were guilty, but he could not condone a lynching.

"I dunno," Elias Hamill's man said dubiously. "Maybe Ryan's right. Maybe we better go to the sheriff."

"We'll go quiet," Tom Wall said. "Honest to God we will."

"Maybe we oughta take 'em in at that," another cowboy said.

Ryan turned toward this new voice of indecision to press his point, but the crew leader was shouting furiously, and some of the others took up the cry: "Hang 'em!" They crowded angrily around Ryan.

"We aren't murderers!" Ryan said, trying to regain his advantage, but it was too late. A blinding light seared his eyes, and he dropped from the saddle into blackness.

In the gathering twilight, Ryan woke with a throbbing headache, his face in the dirt. He dragged himself slowly into consciousness and wiped the mud from his face. He was lying beside a dead fire, and Beau was tethered to a sapling a hundred feet away. Groaning, Ryan sat up and felt the tender lump on the back of his head. Someone had removed him from the argument with the butt of a revolver. He looked up toward the stand of trees on the hill and saw, as he had expected, three dead men, hanging.

Angry and bleak, Ryan staggered to his feet. He would report it, not that it would make much difference. He had not seen who had hit him, or who had lynched the men.

It's too late for this, Ryan thought, looking at the hanged men. *We've come too far to go back to this*.

*　　　*　　　*

They grimly finished the roundup two days later, and by nightfall, Tim Ryan had slogged through a pouring spring rain back to the Broken R.

Swinging himself down from Beau, he leaned his head against his saddle. Aching all over, he felt old. *If this keeps up, I'm gonna look like Dad Henry in a few more years*, he thought. It had rained the last few days they were out on the range; all the men and horses were mud-caked, soaked, and exhausted.

Ryan led Beau into the barn and lit the lantern. The big gray horse shoved his head against Ryan's chest and blew down his wet nose. Ryan shoved him away.

"I want a bath," he told Beau, "but I gotta clean you first, so stand still." Beau snorted at him tolerantly and stuck his nose in the grain bin. Ryan hauled the saddle off and set to work. His head still hurt, and he was heartsick. The memory of the three hanged men haunted him.

After he had finished grooming Beau, he blew out the lantern. The ranch yard was as muddy as the range, and there was a cold wind blowing. He walked across the yard toward the house, where a soft yellow light gleamed in the parlor window. He could see Susannah and Carrie, their faces pressed against the glass, waiting for him. He quickened his step.

On the porch, Tim stopped and cocked his head. He could hear the piano, soft and melodious, playing "My Old Kentucky Home." Caroline had always played that. The front door flew open, and he found himself covered with small girls.

"Papa!"

"Papa, we learned a new song! Do you want to hear it?"

He lifted them up, one at a time, and kissed them. They were too young to remember their mother singing that song, and Mrs. Bradley could not have known it was Caroline's favorite.

He shooed the girls, clad only in long flannel nightgowns, back into the house out of the cold and closed the door. "I'm too dirty to sit down anywhere till I've had a bath. I'll listen afterward. Little Deer!" he shouted. She would heat bath water on the kitchen stove and carry it to the copper tub upstairs.

Elizabeth turned from the piano and smiled at him

gently. The rose china lamps made a golden aureole around
her hair. "The children need to go to bed," she said.
"They were just on their way when we heard all the
commotion outside, so I let them stay up to see you. If
you wait till you've bathed, they'll be asleep on their
feet."

"Oh, all right." Ryan let the girls pull him into the
parlor. Charlie came up in his nightshirt, looking so wistful and glad to see him that Ryan kissed him on the top of
his pale head. "You sing, too?" Ryan asked him.

Charlie nodded. "I know all Mama's songs already," he
said. "But we've been practicing this one. We can't talk to
the piano tuner," Charlie confided, "because he works in
an awful place."

Elizabeth gave a muffled giggle from the piano bench
and started the song over, playing chords until the children settled down.

"You mean you went and got that boy from Meg's?"
Ryan said, startled.

"I did not," Elizabeth said. "Robert Cummings did,
since the gentleman happened to be the only piano tuner
available in this heathen outpost."

Ryan looked closely at her, trying to see if she was
joking with him, and decided that she was. He sat down,
keeping his dirty boots as far away from the furniture as he
could. "Well, go on. Let's hear this masterpiece you've
learned."

Three sweet young voices lifted up, solemnly. Elizabeth
sang with them, just loudly enough to keep them on
the beat. The girls in their nightdresses, their dark
hair brushed into ringlets, stood side by side.

> . . . By an by hard times
> Comes a-knocking at the door,
> Then my old Kentucky home, good night!

"That was nice," Ryan said, as the haunting melody
faded into silence. "Now you go get in bed." He looked
thoughtfully at Elizabeth Bradley, still sitting at the piano,
fingers just touching the polished ivory keys. Then he got
up in a hurry. "Little Deer! You got that water hot yet?"

*   *   *

Somehow, Ryan was never sure how, the cowboys, who had always stayed in the bunkhouse after dinner, began to come to the ranch house instead. First Sam Harkness, hat in hand, wondering if he might just listen to the music. Then Pony Simkins, and John Potter, and then others, even Cal Hodges, until finally there were at least three or four cowboys in the parlor at dusk to watch Elizabeth Bradley light the rose china lamps and listen to her play the piano. At first, Tim had given Mrs. Bradley an apprehensive glance— she had that parlor pretty clean, and he was unsure how she would take to muddy-booted cowboys in it, some of whom chewed tobacco. But she had seemed glad to welcome them, and her only reaction to the tobacco chewing had been to return from her next shopping expedition with a big brass spittoon, which she had placed prominently on the hearth.

Elizabeth knew a lot of songs, some that were familiar to the cowboys and others that were new. She quickly learned to play by ear the ones they taught her. They sang "Red River Valley" and "Sweet Betsy from Pike" and "Seeing Nelly Home." She taught them "Sweet Genevieve" and "Froggy Would A-Wooing Go," which was Charlie's favorite.

Sitting in the parlor one evening, with the smells of spring coming through the open window, hearing the cowboys' voices mingling with his daughters' around Elizabeth's clear guiding notes, Tim Ryan realized that for many of these men this was the first taste of home life they had had since they had left their own homes. In most ranches where cowhands worked there was no woman to make a home, and if there were, she would believe that the cowboys belonged in the bunkhouse, not the parlor. His wife, Caroline, would rather have welcomed a longhorn steer into her parlor.

Ryan watched Sam Harkness, who sat with little Carrie on his knee. Sam had stopped mooning over Mrs. Bradley and had begun to court Lily Cummings's Swedish bound girl. Carrie and Sam joined in with the other voices:

When the mistletoe was green
    Midst the winter snows,

Sunshine in thy face was seen,
  Kissing lips of rose.
Aura Lea, Aura Lea,
  Take my golden ring;
Love and light return with thee,
  And swallows with the spring.

The rose china lamps cast their soft glow over the parlor. Elizabeth, with Susannah and Charlie on either side of her, played liltingly. There was a bowl of prairie wildflowers on the marble-topped table, and there had been apple pie for dinner. Ryan chuckled. No wonder Sam was so eager to get married.

The next day, Tim Ryan rode into Shawnee to see about hiring more hands for the trail drive to Omaha. He was not going on the drive himself—John Potter was the best trail boss around—and Ryan would need most of his men on the ranch. When he arrived in town, he saw the Broken R buggy hitched outside Fishburn's store. He realized he had forgotten to tell Mrs. Bradley to pick up some salt lick, so he hitched Beau beside the buggy and went in.

Inside, he found Mrs. Bradley discussing the opera with George Bigelow. *Prattling away like a damned fool*, Ryan thought sourly, while Bigelow stood there listening, looking smarmy.

"We do get an opera in Shawnee now and then," Bigelow was saying, "but unfortunately the performers are not generally what you would call specialists in the art." He smiled. "The last troupe, as I recall, also played in the pantomime and, I believe, built the scenery."

Elizabeth saw Tim Ryan over Bigelow's shoulder. "Good morning," she said cheerily. "I came for the sugar and coffee, and some goods to make the girls new pinafores. Is there anything I can take back for you?"

"Yeah," Ryan growled. "Six ten-pound blocks of salt lick." He looked at Joe Fishburn, who was standing behind the counter. "Just stick it in the wagon," he muttered and stalked out.

Elizabeth looked after him, with a sinking feeling. Tim Ryan was furious because he had seen her talking to

George Bigelow. He probably thought she had gone into town specifically to meet Bigelow. *Well, did you?* she asked herself. They had needed sugar and coffee, and the girls sorely needed pinafores, but she had to face the truth that she had also been thinking about George Bigelow. She was almost certain that he was going to propose to her, and she wanted to decide what she was going to say before the subject came up. She was afraid she might say the first thing that came to mind just because she was angry with Tim Ryan.

Why she should be angry with Tim Ryan most of the time, Elizabeth was not sure. She suspected, when she was honest with herself, that she was attracted to him, while he was obviously not interested in her. He had all the enticing qualities of forbidden fruit.

George Bigelow, Elizabeth told herself firmly, was just as handsome as Tim Ryan, and he was interested. He brought her appropriate presents—candy, flowers, and, most valuable on the prairie, books. Tim Ryan, on the other hand, had given her a parlor-house cow that she had to milk at four A.M. And, Elizabeth thought, as Bigelow paid for his purchases and handed her a sack of candy for the children, Bigelow did not criticize her, something that could not be said of Tim Ryan. She took the candy and smiled gratefully at Bigelow.

George Bigelow whistled cheerily as he left. At the door he bumped into Emma Lang. He raised his hat and gave her a sharklike smile. Emma slouched past him, her thin face weary and preoccupied. She saw Elizabeth and brightened.

"Mrs. Bradley, you tell Mr. Ryan how grateful we are, Monty and me, for the men he sent over to help with the barn. Wasn't for them, I don't know what we'd of done."

Elizabeth took her hands. Emma Lang was nothing but a child. She looked even younger than she had at church. "I know Mr. Ryan was glad to help in any way he could. Are you getting along all right now?"

Emma sighed and looked at her toes. She had on heavy work boots, and the hem of her faded calico dress was crusted with mud. She looked up at Elizabeth's friendly, sympathetic face. "We get along all right, I guess," she mumbled aloud.

"Is something wrong?" Elizabeth asked gently. The young woman looked miserable.

"The Lord says we mustn't be dissatisfied." Emma sighed again. "But I envy you, I purely do."

"Envy me?" Elizabeth said, startled. Here, as everywhere, an unmarried woman had little social status. "Why, Mrs. Lang, I'm only a housekeeper. You have a husband and land of your own!"

"At least you get paid!" Emma blurted and burst into tears.

"Mrs. Lang—Emma—" Elizabeth looked helplessly at Elvina Fishburn, who just shrugged her shoulders. "Here, come and sit down." Elizabeth put her arm around the young woman's shoulders and led her to two wooden chairs near the window.

"I know I oughtn't to be telling you my troubles," Emma sobbed. "It ain't fittin', but sometimes I feel like if I don't talk to somebody I just plain can't go on. Ma says that's the way the world's always been and a wife's got to abide by her husband. And Pa says I made my bed, now I gotta lie in it. I don't want much—God knows we never had much at home—and I love Monty, I truly do, but sometimes I want—I don't know," she wailed, "just somethin' more. Monty can't think about anything but gettin' ahead, and now that the barn got burnt, he's worse than ever, tryin' to put every penny by. And I'm good at it, I truly am; Ma taught me how to keep household. But just sometimes . . ."

She put her face in her hands, her shoulders quivering, while Elizabeth helplessly stroked her back. "I bought a hair ribbon," Emma sobbed. "A pretty red one, just to look nice. There was three cents left over from the flour an' beans, and that bit of ribbon was so pretty. I'm not supposed to buy anything Monty doesn't tell me to get, and he—he spanked me. If I'd wanted that," she sniffled, "I coulda stayed home with Pa. I know we don't have no money to waste, but I ain't a kid. I work just as hard as he does. I know he don't spend nothing on himself either, but what did he marry me for, if he thinks I'm a kid?"

Elizabeth's mouth tightened. That Monty Lang ought to be ashamed of himself. *Men!* she thought and glared balefully at Joe Fishburn, the only male available, including him in her general condemnation.

That evening, Tim Ryan looked up from the Broken R's account books to find Mrs. Bradley on the other side of his desk, regarding him with a look of indignant determination.

"Mr. Ryan, I must speak with you," she said.

"What have they done now?" he inquired warily. Carrie and Susannah were capable of anything, he had found, but he thought Mrs. Bradley now had them in control. He was uncomfortably aware that Mrs. Bradley had on her nightdress, with a woolen wrapper over it. She looked so soft, so different from the stiff, corseted formality that was her daytime self.

"It isn't the children," Elizabeth said. She realized that he was looking at more than her face, and she folded her arms across her chest.

Tim Ryan dropped his eyes hastily to his account books. "Then what is it?" he said gruffly.

"I waited until this evening in order to speak to you privately," Elizabeth said. "I met Emma Lang in Fishburn's today." She briskly told him of her conversation with Emma.

Ryan put his pen down. "Now don't you get mixed up in other folks' private business. Monty Lang is a good man, and you haven't got any idea what goes on between him and his wife. He's doing his best to build a future out here, and if he's tight with a dollar, I'm not surprised."

"Monty Lang can afford a three-cent hair ribbon!" Elizabeth snapped. "And I have an excellent idea of what goes on. That child was in tears. Monty Lang needs to learn how to treat a wife."

"Now, Mrs. Bradley, it's not my business to tell him."

"He's your friend," Elizabeth said.

"Now, Mrs. Bradley, you're getting all worked up—"

"Quit saying 'Now, Mrs. Bradley' in that patronizing tone, as if I were a horse," Elizabeth said. Her blue eyes did not blink for a few moments, and she stared at him.

"Emma's young, and they haven't been married six months," Ryan said. The blue eyes continued to stare at him implacably. "Things will shake themselves out and settle down. You'll see. The first year is always the hardest."

"Emma may be young, but Monty Lang is twenty-nine if he's a day, and he's old enough to know better," Elizabeth said. "Turning your wife over your knee should have gone out with the Dark Ages! My late husband would never have done such a thing."

"Well, he probably couldn't duck very fast, what with his wound," Ryan said with spurious sympathy. "I wouldn't be surprised if you had a good arm with a rolling pin."

Elizabeth, seething, looked about her for something to throw, and Ryan quickly slid an onyx ruler from her reach. Suddenly her lip twitched, and she caught a flicker of answering amusement in Ryan's cat-green eyes. "I have never had occasion to find out, Mr. Ryan," she said sweetly, "since no man has ever attempted to take such liberties with me."

"I'll bet," Tim Ryan said. Even with those cornflower-blue eyes and that gold hair all braided for the night, she gave the impression of being able to wield a worse weapon than a rolling pin if the need arose. "Now, why don't you think Emma Lang can take care of herself, too?" he asked.

"Because she's young," Elizabeth said. "And because she's probably not as stubborn as I am."

"Mrs. Bradley," Ryan said, "nobody is as stubborn as you are."

"You know I'm right," Elizabeth said. "If Monty Lang wants a partner, instead of a terrified, resentful slave, he'd better change his ways. Mr. Ryan, you can't tell me you ever would have struck your own wife in that degrading fashion."

The laughter died suddenly in Ryan's eyes. He did not speak.

"I'm sorry," she said softly. "I shouldn't have brought up—"

"It's all right," he said brusquely. "Now, I've got accounts to finish. Don't you worry about Emma Lang. If that hair ribbon is the worst of her troubles, she'll have a better marriage than most folks."

"Yes," Elizabeth said, thinking of most folks' marriages. "But it seems a shame that she has to settle for that." She turned and left, her blond braid swinging behind her.

Tim Ryan sighed and put his hat on. It was just eight o'clock, and there was a full moon. Not too late to ride out to Monty Lang's place.

As he stalked down the porch steps into the yard, he turned and glared back at the house. *Blast that meddling Mrs. Bradley and her notions about marriage,* he thought; but he went out to the barn and saddled up Beau. If Monty Lang ended up as miserable as Tim Ryan had been, it was not going to be Ryan's fault.

Chapter Six

The next morning breakfast was served at four, and Elizabeth and the sleepy-eyed children stumbled into the dining room to say good-bye to John Potter. They watched the extra hands hired for the trail drive gather in the gray predawn outside the house. The sound of lowing cattle filled the air, and as the sun crept up, they could see shaggy, moving shapes on the open prairie beyond the corrals, a great live blanket of longhorns under a cloud of dust.

"You take care of the boss, now, while I'm gone." John Potter tweaked the little girls' pigtails gently and bent down while they each kissed him on the cheek. Charlie, his nose pressed against the window, was watching the men outside. John Potter put his hand on Charlie's shoulder. "You get a little bigger, young 'un, and I'll take you with me."

"Yes, sir! How big do I have to get?"

John Potter considered that. "About up to here." He held his hand a foot over Charlie's head.

When the trail drive moved out, Charlie stood on the front porch for nearly an hour, watching until they were out of sight.

Elizabeth looked at her son as the girls joined him. *He needs a father*, she thought. *I'm not enough.* She went out onto the porch and put an arm around Charlie sympathetically. "Come on," she said. "I'll saddle Jericho and ride to school with you."

"Want some company, little housekeeper?" Elizabeth turned to find Cal Hodges on the porch behind her. "Might get kinda lonesome ridin' back by yourself."

Elizabeth ignored him, coldly. She had come to detest Cal Hodges.

"Whatsa matter? You got better prospects than me waitin' for you in town?" Cal's leer was suggestive and unpleasant.

"Get to work!" Tim Ryan slammed the front door behind him, and Cal lazily pulled his hat over his eyes and sauntered toward the barn. Ryan looked at Elizabeth. "Does he bother you?"

Elizabeth was determined she was not going to make any further trouble for Tim Ryan. "No," she muttered. "Not exactly."

Ryan glanced at her sideways, and his eyes slid away again. She looked so natural there on the porch with the children gathered around her—too much like Caroline. "Well, you tell me if he does. Now you kids go on and get to school."

In spite of himself, Ryan watched her as they rode away, her black skirts bunched up indecorously about her knees, her slim legs clad in long black stockings. Pretty disreputable for a staid old widow woman, he thought and chuckled. He would bet she had never ridden anything but a sidesaddle before she came to Wyoming. But she was adaptable; he had to give her credit for that.

"Hey, boss, you got company!"

Ryan turned his head around. Sam Harkness was pointing north across the waving prairie grass at a solitary rider approaching them.

"Injun!" Cal Hodges said. He spat, and his fingers moved toward the holster on his hip.

"Put that away!" Ryan snapped.

"I don't trust Injuns."

"You get to work," Ryan ordered. He looked at the other men in the yard. "If I see one sign of trouble from any of you while he's here, you're off this place."

"Sure, boss." They watched the rider curiously.

Cal unhitched his horse, a big pinto, and swung into the

saddle. "I don't like Injuns," he said. He kicked the horse and rode off in the opposite direction.

Ryan watched him go with relief.

As the rider drew closer, Ryan raised a hand in greeting. The Indian lifted his own in return. In a moment, he drew rein in the yard and sat, looking solemnly at Tim Ryan. "I thought you had gone with them." He pointed in the direction the trail drive had taken. "You are growing lazy, Ryan." A quick, unexpected grin split his dark face.

"What's the point in being the boss if you can't make somebody else do the work?" Ryan said.

Chief Black Wolf shook his head. "I find, my friend, that being the boss means that you do what no one else will." He swung himself down from his pony's back, and Ryan beckoned him indoors. The piebald pony stood obediently where Black Wolf had left it, snuffling among the few blades of grass in the yard. It carried no saddle except a red and white blanket, and its bridle was a bitless halter of braided rawhide thongs, with a knot of red feathers on the headstall.

Ryan motioned Black Wolf into the house. As they passed the kitchen door, Little Deer averted her eyes, and Black Wolf pretended not to have seen her.

In his office, Ryan drew up two red leather chairs and sat down facing Black Wolf. "You've come a long way for a game of chess," he said. It was a pastime he had taught Black Wolf long ago, and one that they both enjoyed, though he did not really believe that was the reason for the visit.

"And a long way on dangerous ground," Black Wolf added. A lone white man on Indian land was in as much danger as a lone Indian on the cattleman's range. "But there is wickedness in the wind, so I came."

Ryan's eyes narrowed. "Tell me what has happened, Black Wolf."

"Your government has pushed my people back and back," Black Wolf said. "Now we will back up no farther. Not me alone, but others—many, many of us—have decided this. You tell this to the men who graze their cattle on our hunting grounds."

"That land is yours by treaty," Ryan said.

"When has a treaty stopped men's greed?" Black Wolf replied. "The white men are trying to make a war over this land, so that the government will send soldiers to help them take it from us."

"There isn't going to be any war," Ryan said flatly, nevertheless realizing that he could not guarantee it. With the homesteaders pushing their way into the cattle ranges, every rancher in Wyoming had begun to look covetously at the Sioux lands to the north. And what the white man coveted, he had so far found a way to take. "Why do you say the white men are trying to make war?"

"They make small troubles in our hunting grounds. They provoke quarrels with my braves, who are prideful and hotheaded. The white men do not attack. They taunt us in the hope that we will attack, and then they will have reason to call on the soldiers. It will not matter who is in the right, my friend. If the soldiers come, there will be no stopping it."

"What white men?"

"I do not know them. I do not like white men, saving you. I come here because I think perhaps that you know them and can stop them."

"And if I can't?" Ryan asked.

"Then I will not be able to stop my young men," Black Wolf said. "I do not think we can win a war. If I did, I tell you, my friend, I would make one. But we can make it very costly for the white man to win one. Very costly. You will tell this to the rest."

Ryan nodded. "I will tell them."

"Tell them also that the next one provoking my braves in their hunting grounds may come back across his saddle." He stood up and went to the glass-fronted bookcase where Ryan kept his chessmen. "And now I will play you a game anyway." Black Wolf put the chess set on the table between them and sat down again. His dark hair hung in two braids over his shoulders. The hawk's feather knotted into one braid cast a shadow like a knife blade across the board.

*   *   *

When Black Wolf rode away two hours later, Ryan stood looking after him thoughtfully. The chief had risked a great deal to come, Ryan knew, not the least of which was the lessening of his standing in his braves' eyes by going to a white man for help against other white men.

Pony Simkins broke into Ryan's thoughts as he scurried across the yard toward him, his weatherbeaten face wrinkled in a worried frown.

"That dog of yours is gettin' ready to whelp," Simkins said, "and she don't look good to me."

"Where is she?"

"In the barn."

Ryan trotted across the yard and found Frieda stretched out in the hay, her flanks heaving. Her eyes looked dull and glassy, and there were white flecks of foam around her mouth. "Damn!" Ryan felt the pups bulging against her side and sat back helplessly on his heels.

"She's in a bad way." He stood up. "I'm gonna take her to Meg. She's the closest thing we've got to a vet out here. Where's Mrs. Bradley?"

"She just got back from riding the kids to school," Simkins said.

"Tell her to get me a clean blanket." Ryan took Elizabeth's saddle off Jericho and began to hitch him to the buggy.

Elizabeth came in clutching a blanket a few moments later. "Poor thing. Do you want me to go with you? Where are you taking her?"

"To Meg Callahan," Ryan said, lifting Frieda onto the blanket. The dog moaned softly as he moved her. "And, no, I don't want you to come with me, not if you want to be able to show your face in Shawnee again."

"Oh," Elizabeth said. She stroked Frieda's head and then got out of the way as Ryan shook out Jericho's reins. He drove off with no further comment.

"He's got a good heart," Pony Simkins said as the buggy rattled out of the yard. "Most folks wouldn't bother."

A good heart where hapless Indians, and friends like Monty Lang, and children and dogs were concerned. It was a pity, Elizabeth thought, that it did not extend to her.

*   *   *

Tim Ryan marched into Meg's establishment in the middle of the noonday meal with the pregnant Frieda in his arms.

"Don't look at me," Clyde Sawyer said. "I ain't the father."

"You shut up," Ryan said when the guffaws had died down, "or I'll tell Agnes you're here. Meg, she needs help. I don't know what I'm doing."

"Take her to my office," Meg said, getting up from the table.

Ryan pushed through the swinging door that led to the back of the house, and Meg followed him, pausing to grab a canvas apron from a hook in the kitchen. She tied it over her expensive bronze-green silk dress and pushed her sleeves up to her elbows. Ryan put Frieda on the blanket, on the floor, and Meg examined her. Howler got up from his nap on the settee and sniffed at Frieda sympathetically.

"Go tell Louis to get me some boiled water and some clean sheets and towels," Meg said to Ryan.

Louis was the cook, and temperamental, but not when the orders came from Meg. Ryan found him in the kitchen feeding pound cake to the raccoon. As Louis went to get the sheets, Ryan looked at the raccoon. It had a piece of cake sticking out of the corner of its mouth. "You're in clover, you know that," he told it.

Ryan took the sheets and the water from Louis when he returned, and went back to Meg's office. It was elegant and businesslike, with a big carved oak desk and a safe. There was a Persian carpet on the floor.

"Spread those sheets on my rug," Meg said.

"Is she gonna be all right?"

"How do I know yet?" Meg muttered. "She's got a big pup in there, and he's turned sideways."

"Can I help?"

"You can stay out of my hair." Meg gave him a look of exasperated affection and bent over Frieda again. "What did she mate with, a buffalo?"

"How the hell do I know?" Ryan said. He gave Howler a look. "I got my suspicions."

"Attagirl," Meg murmured to the dog. "You're gettin' there." She looked up at Ryan. "Go eat lunch or something."

He wandered into the dining room.

"You gonna hand out cigars, Ryan?" Clyde Sawyer asked him.

"Shut up."

Sadie and Lucy looked at Ryan hopefully, but he sat down at the table and cut himself a slice of ham. After a few minutes he got up, paced restlessly through the parlor, and then went back to Meg's office. Meg, her apron and arms stained with blood, was on her knees next to the dog. There was a pup on the floor beside her. "Now you can help," she said. "Get me my scissors."

Ryan handed them to her. "Pinch the cord here." She cut the umbilical cord and tied it. "Wrap him up in that towel. He was the problem. I think we're all right now."

All the same, it took another three hours to deliver the pups. There were six of them, and Frieda was too worn out to help. When they were through, Ryan and Meg were covered in blood, and Meg's gown was ruined.

"I owe you a dress," Ryan said. "She's a good dog. I wouldn't have wanted to lose her."

"You may lose this one," Meg said. She was lining the pups up to nurse. The smallest one made feeble whimpers but did not seem to know what to do. The others pushed it aside ruthlessly. "It's gonna have to be bottle fed," Meg said. "You think maybe your housekeeper . . . ?"

"No," he said flatly. "She's got enough to do."

Meg raised her eyebrows.

"She'd do it," Ryan muttered. "I just don't want to be beholden."

Meg looked at him thoughtfully. "She gettin' along all right out here?" she asked, trying to sound casual. "City woman and all?"

"Yeah, fine," Ryan answered.

Something had closed in his face when she had brought up Mrs. Bradley, Meg realized. *I knew it.* She felt like crying. *He's fallen in love with her. He was bound to. He won't admit it, and she'll go and marry George Bigelow and break his heart.*

Meg heard all the gossip. She had heard enough to

know that Elizabeth Bradley was nothing like Caroline Ryan except in looks. But it was those looks, and having been burned once, that were going to break Tim Ryan's heart. And her own heart, as well, Meg thought ruefully.

She sat back and picked up the little pup. "I'll keep him for you, Tim, and see if I can't get him to eat." She smiled wanly at Ryan, her hair limply curling around her tired face. "You can call it Howler's stud fee."

"I thought I was supposed to pay you."

Meg chuckled. "Would you?"

"Not on your life. What do I want with a wolf?"

"Make you a better guard dog than this silly bitch." Meg looked at Frieda with affection. "You might give 'em to a few homesteaders," she added soberly. "I was gonna send somebody out to your place with a note, but this emergency with the dog made me forget." She pulled her apron off and sat down in the big swivel chair at her desk. "There were a couple of cowboys in here this morning. Drunk at ten o'clock and shooting off their mouths. Something's going on that I don't like."

"What?" Ryan's eyes narrowed as he considered his conversation with Black Wolf.

"Hired guns," Meg said with disgust. "Enforcers, they called 'em. They were talkin' to each other, thought I wasn't listening."

"Did you tell the sheriff? I better talk to him." Ryan thought that Sheriff Henry Purchase would need some prodding. Henry did not like to go against the cattlemen, and he had no liking for Indians.

"Hank?" Meg laughed. "You don't think he'd stick around with trouble brewing, do you? He took off yesterday to collect land fees on the other side of the county, and he didn't deputize anybody to watch things while he was away, either. Hank knows which side his bread's buttered on."

Ryan nodded grimly. The cattlemen had got Henry Purchase appointed. Ryan had tried to find a better candidate—an act that had not endeared him to the other cattlemen—but no one with any sense wanted to go against the big ranchers' choice.

"Black Wolf came in to see me this morning," Ryan told

her. "He thinks something's coming, too. Those damn fools are trying to start a war."

"If they are," Meg said, "I don't think it's with the Indians. I think they're after homesteaders. I didn't hear much, because they stopped talking as soon as they saw me."

"What exactly did you hear?"

Meg frowned. "He said, 'They'll run that squatter and his brat bride outta the county.' Doesn't sound like the Indians to me."

An image of a barn in flames flashed through Ryan's mind. "Whose men were they?" he asked.

"One of 'em I'd never seen before," Meg answered. "People hire a lot of extra hands this time of year. But I think I saw the other one before, workin' for George Bigelow."

"Goddamn it!" Ryan got up in a hurry. He was certain this man was still working for Bigelow, but a conversation overheard in a whorehouse was not enough evidence to convince the sheriff that Bigelow was responsible. "When's Hank due back?"

"Tomorrow," Meg said.

That meant that if there was going to be trouble, it would occur tonight. He looked at Frieda and the pups. "Help me get her in the buggy. Those bastards are going to get a surprise."

After they had put the dogs on the buggy floor, Ryan waved good-bye and whipped Jericho to a gallop. He was almost sure he knew where the hired guns were heading, and he hoped he was going to be in time.

While Tim Ryan was delivering puppies at Meg Callahan's, Elizabeth drove the wagon back into town. She had decided to meet the children after school and needed the time to cool her temper. Tim Ryan seemed to get under her skin with every word he spoke. She had had no intention of going to Meg Callahan's parlor house with him, Elizabeth thought irritably, and he had had no reason to answer her so abruptly. The way he had put it had left her feeling like a fool. When she got to the schoolhouse, she was an hour early, so she drove into Shawnee to Fishburn's store to browse and buy the children some peppermints.

George Bigelow was in Fishburn's, trying on a new hat. He beamed when he saw Elizabeth. "Mrs. Bradley! Just the arbiter of fashion I require. How do I look?" He struck a pose, head held high, one hand on his hip.

"Dashing, Mr. Bigelow. A perfect hat. You should buy it." Elizabeth felt her irritable mood fading. She had always liked a man with whom she could joke.

"I shall buy it immediately." Bigelow gave Elvina Fishburn the money, while Elizabeth watched him wistfully. Bigelow smiled at her. "I am sure your advice is sound, Mrs. Bradley."

"Oh, it is, Mr. Bigelow," she assured him.

Bigelow turned away from the counter. "I don't suppose you could bring yourself to call me George," he suggested.

"No, Mr. Bigelow." But she smiled at him, that dazzling smile. "Not just yet."

"Then there is hope." He looked at her, the smile still curving up the corners of his mouth. "I shall take that to heart."

Elizabeth edged a little farther away from the counter. She knew Elvina Fishburn was taking notes. "You may take it that I have my reputation to look after," she said demurely.

"Of course," Bigelow said. He bent his head a little closer to hers. "I could always be George in private," he suggested.

"I suppose you could," Elizabeth agreed. She cocked her head up at him. "But not, Mr. Bigelow, until you are also George in public."

"Naturally," Bigelow said. He tipped the new hat to her and departed, whistling. Mrs. Bradley had made it as plain as a lady could make it that she would consider an offer of marriage, but not an offer of anything else. That was all right. It was marriage he had in mind, and George Bigelow's wife must be above reproach.

And why, Elizabeth thought as George left, did she feel so leaden? She had encouraged him intentionally. George Bigelow made her feel admired, courted—desirable.

"George Bigelow's a solid man in Shawnee," Elvina Fishburn commented from behind the counter. "Gonna be governor of the territory one of these days, I reckon."

"I shouldn't wonder," Elizabeth said absently. She thought George Bigelow could probably be whatever he put his mind to.

"A woman could do a lot worse." Elvina leaned her elbows on the counter. "Plenty of gals have set their caps for George, but I guess they ain't been what he had in mind."

"That's hardly my concern," Elizabeth said. She did not want to insult Elvina Fishburn, but whether she married George Bigelow or not, she did not want him to find out she had been gossiping about him in Fishburn's store. "I'll have a nickel's worth of those good peppermints of yours," she added as the bell over the door jingled behind her. While Elvina scooped peppermints into a sack, Elizabeth turned to find Emma Lang smiling at her.

"Mrs. Lang, how nice to see you." The child looked happier; there was a light in her eyes that had not been there yesterday.

"You call me Emma," she said.

"All right, dear. And you must call me Elizabeth."

"Can I? I don't feel grown up enough to be 'Mrs. Lang'," she confided. "Today I been trying, though, and I reckon I got you to thank for that. I need a sack of ten-penny nails, and some calico for curtains," she told Elvina Fishburn proudly. "The red. I do like red."

"Me to thank?" Elizabeth said, puzzled.

"Well, you told Mr. Ryan about what I told you in here yesterday, didn't you?" Emma said, her eyes dancing. "And you know what he done? He sat my Monty down and read him a lecture like a Dutch uncle, that's what he done. And afterward, Monty said he was sorry, and we talked, musta been till the middle of the night. We ain't never done that before. Monty said he was gonna try to remember I wasn't nothing but a kid yet. And he was so sweet I got to thinking about all that he's done for us, building up the place like he's done, and I said if I was gonna be a married lady I reckoned it was time I quit being a kid. And I said I was sorry about the hair ribbon, and next time I had three cents to spare I was gonna buy tobacco for him. And he laughed and laughed. And now he's gonna build me some shelves for the dishes, and we're putting up curtains."

Emma Lang's bright eyes looked at Elizabeth gratefully. "It's a whole new day, and I do thank you."

"I'm so glad things have worked out for you," Elizabeth said. "But don't thank me. You and Monty did it. You just needed a little push, perhaps, and Mr. Ryan seems to be the one who provided that."

So much for Tim Ryan's lectures on staying out of other people's business, Elizabeth thought with affection as she drove the wagon back toward the schoolhouse. He was a good man, in spite of the way he acted sometimes. She tried to imagine George Bigelow giving an erring husband a fatherly talk, and found she could not.

It was nearly dark when she drove into the ranch yard, the children behind her on their ponies. Tim Ryan, riding out with Sam Harkness, Pony Simkins, and two other men, flew past her. They were fast-moving shadows in the yard.

"What's the matter?" she called after him, but she had no answer except for the spatter of their hoofbeats, fading in the darkness.

Chapter Seven

Emma Lang came home with her calico to find Monty waiting for her, sitting on the apple crate under the slanting roof of the front porch. She jumped down from the wagon, and he came up and swung her into his arms.

"You find yourself some pretty stuff?" He looked over her shoulder at the paper-wrapped parcel on the wagon seat.

"Pretty red calico," Emma said. "The prettiest you ever saw. Oh, Monty, it's gonna look like a house now!"

She beamed at him in the dusk, and he bent his head and kissed her. After a minute his hands started to rove.

Emma giggled. "Monty, that's not decent! Out here in the open!"

"Who's gonna see us? The cows? They got their own business to tend to." He grinned down at her, not letting go. "Might be a sight more comfortable in the house, though," he suggested.

"I gotta cook your supper," Emma protested.

"I ain't hungry. Not for supper. I cut all the wood for your shelves while you were gone," he said. "Ain't you gonna be grateful?"

Emma laid her head against his chest. "Aw, you know I am. I guess supper could wait. But what would my ma say . . . ?"

"I ain't married to your ma," Monty chuckled. He felt fine. Tim Ryan was right. What was the point of being

96

married if you didn't take time—and a few pennies—to make it fun? He kept one arm around her waist as they walked to the cabin.

Inside, the cabin was warm, cozy, and a little smoky from the fire Monty had kindled in the hearth. He untied the string of Emma's cloak and started unbuttoning her dress. Emma protested halfheartedly. It still did not seem decent to make love before supper, but if Monty wanted to . . .

She let him pull her dress over her head and untie her chemise.

Monty ran his hands over his wife's trim body. She just giggled and let him pick her up and drop her on the pretty pieced quilt that had been part of her wedding linen.

He lay down on top of her, enjoying the feel of her close to him. "I swear I ain't never going to lay a hand on you again, 'cept this way," he whispered.

"I reckon you might, if you get good and mad. You ain't no saint, Monty Lang," Emma whispered back. "But next time I'm gonna hit back. Or I'm gonna pick up a rolling pin, and I reckon that'll settle that."

"I reckon it will," Monty said. He kissed her and snuggled his face in the hollow of her throat. Emma wrapped her arms around him and sighed contentedly.

He kissed her again, but then raised his head suddenly, intent, listening.

"What is it?" Emma's eyes opened wide in fright as she remembered the barn.

"I don't know. Nothing maybe." But he rolled off the bed. "Get dressed!" he whispered.

Emma tied the strings of her chemise with shaking fingers. Now she thought she heard something, but it was hard to tell whether it was just the cattle moving around or their own horses. Monty was already at the door, with the shotgun in his hands. He went out, closing the door behind him. Emma wriggled into her dress, buttoning it in a hurry, wrenching a button off in her panic. She threw a shawl over her shoulders and looked around for Monty's Colt. She heard voices outside now, indistinguishable menacing rumbles. She found the Colt and pulled the door open, holding the heavy gun in both hands.

In the yard were men on horses, their hats pulled low over their eyes and bandannas covering their mouths.

"Get off my land," Monty said. He raised the shotgun.

"You got it wrong, squatter. You're the one that's goin' to get off this land. You an' that squatter's brat you married. You're gonna take your clothes and get, cow thief."

The faint light from the cabin window glittered on their guns. Emma could see six of them, too many for the two of them.

"Nobody calls me a thief." Monty's voice grated with anger.

"They can call you a dead thief if you don't do it." A rope swung from the speaker's hand.

"No!" Emma stepped up beside Monty, leveling the Colt.

"Get in the house!" Monty snapped at her.

"Put down that gun, girl." The men inched their horses closer.

"Goddamn you, get offa my land!" Monty said.

One of the men laughed. "Like I told you, it ain't your land." He reached into a sack hanging from his saddle and pulled out a can of kerosene. "We're just gonna do a little brush clearin'. If you wanna keep your clothes, girl, you better go get 'em."

"Someone's comin'!" one of the other men said suddenly.

The man with the kerosene jerked his head around, then turned back to Monty. "You just stand right there, squatter." He swung his horse around a little and peered across the porch into the night.

Emma could hear hoofbeats now. She stared into the darkness, shaking, and then gasped in relief at the sound of a familiar voice.

"Monty?" Tim Ryan's voice called through the darkness. "Are you all right?"

"Watch your step, Tim," Monty said evenly. "There's some rattlesnakes out tonight."

"Yeah, I can see that." With his own men behind him, Ryan drew rein and surveyed the six intruders. "You go back and tell your boss we don't hold with your kind in this county."

"And who the hell might you be?"

"Name's Ryan. I own the spread over the creek." Whoever hired these men would have told them to steer clear of Tim Ryan.

"Yeah, I heard about you. You're the one who's soft on squatters, ain't you? Well, I don't see no reason for you to stick your nose in what ain't your business."

"I'm making it my business."

"Yeah, you got a reputation for that, too. Well, we're aimin' to clear out this nest of squatters, so you just back off and won't nobody get hurt." The man glanced at Monty. "Long as this cattle thief behaves himself." His eyes flicked toward Emma. "You waited too long, girl. Reckon you can walk outta here with the clothes on your back, now." He lifted the kerosene can.

"I'll shoot every damn one of you before I let you lay a hand to my house!" Monty cocked the shotgun.

"That's a shame." The man with the rope spoke again, lifting a noose. "Your little lady's just liable to get shot for your pains, and we can still take care o' you later."

Monty pulled Emma behind him, lifted the shotgun, and fired. While the gunshot rang through the night, Tim Ryan's men drew their weapons, and the harsh, terrible sound of gunfire reverberated throughout the yard.

It was dark and difficult to see. The first shots slammed into the front wall of the house just as Monty shoved Emma through the door. The gun muzzles seemed to spit flame, and the sound rang with hellish intensity across the still prairie. Monty flattened himself on the porch floor and fired the shotgun at the intruders, who had pulled back when Ryan's men returned their fire.

The hired gunmen spun their horses around and vanished behind the barn. Then a flash in the blackness told Monty that one of them had come back to drop down behind the watering trough. Monty inched forward on the porch and saw another man dart like a ghost from behind the barn. Monty fired, but he was an instant too late, and the man dropped behind the trough along with the first man. Their horses must be tethered somewhere beyond the barn, Monty thought.

A bullet split Emma's apple crate two feet from Monty. Ryan fired back at the flash and dropped from Beau's saddle before the gunmen could get his measure in turn. He smacked Beau on the rump and sent him trotting out of the way.

"Scatter!" Ryan shouted to his men. He began inching along the side of the house, hoping to come at the gunmen from the other side. He thought about that can of kerosene, which had fallen to the ground as the first shots were fired. He and his men had to keep the intruders pinned down so they would not find it and use it.

Ryan slunk along the side of the house under the eaves, not knowing where the gunmen were, except for the two behind the trough, and uncertain where his own men were. He wondered how much he showed against the rough logs of Monty's cabin.

Then a shot sank into the logs beside him. Ryan dropped and rolled back frantically for cover under the porch, while Monty fired just above him.

"We're still gonna burn you out, squatter!" one of the gunmen shouted from the darkness. "But we're gonna hang you first!"

"Come and get me, you son of a bitch!" Monty yelled.

"Shut up, you idiot," Ryan hissed at him. "They're marking where you are."

In the house the noise was deafening, hammering at Emma from all sides. A shadow went past the window, and she lifted the Colt, unsure whether it was Tim Ryan's man or not. She faced the door, ready to fire if it proved to be one of the hired gunmen.

Suddenly the door slammed open, and Pony Simkins burst through. He pushed the terrified Emma down onto the floor. "I can see you plain as day in that window, just like a target," Simkins said. "Now get down and stay down."

"It's my house, too!" Emma gasped.

"I'll argue with you later," Simkins said. "Hang onto that gun, but stay on the floor!" He dived through the door again, slamming it behind him, and leaped the porch railing as a shot went over his head. Simkins hit the ground rolling, scrambled up, and kept going on hands and knees until he was in the barred shadows of the corral fence. He eased his way along the fence line on his belly, propped himself up on his elbows, and took a good look at the barn. He was beginning to get his night vision. Just at the corner of the barn, he spotted a humped shape breaking the straight line of the wall.

Another flurry of gunfire cracked through the night. Simkins ignored it and took careful aim. He fired, and the figure by the barn yelped and staggered away from the wall.

One of the men behind the watering trough jerked his head up, startled into incaution. Tim Ryan fired from beneath the porch, and the man heaved forward and fell over the trough, arms trailing into the water. The gunman beside the dead man scrambled to his feet and ran as Sam Harkness came around the corner of the house, reloading frantically. Ryan's other two men, Bill Ennis and Julio Reyes, fired at the retreating form.

"Pull back! Get outta here!" someone shouted. The gunmen scrambled for their horses. They were getting paid to burn out a squatter and his wife; a gunfight with Tim Ryan and his men had not been in the bargain. Now that the odds were badly against them, they wheeled their horses into the darkness beyond the barn, and a riderless animal galloped after them.

Sam Harkness flung himself into the saddle and urged his horse after them. Pony Simkins, on foot, ran behind him. The fleeing gunmen fired a volley at them.

"Get back here!" Ryan shouted. In the darkness he could not see Sam lurch in his saddle, but Sam's horse slowed to a walk.

Pony Simkins turned around reluctantly. "I coulda had one of 'em!" he argued.

"And he could've had you," Ryan said. "You'll get your chance if they're stupid enough to come back." He eased himself out from under the porch and looked up. "Monty, you all right?"

Monty stood up slowly. "Yeah . . . Emma!" He bolted for the door.

"I'm all right." Emma had eased the door open. The Colt hung in her hand.

"Give me that!" Monty snatched it away from her. "Baby, you're a damn fool." Relieved, he pulled her into his arms.

"Hey, boss!" Bill Ennis shouted from the darkness.

Ryan turned just as Sam Harkness slid silently down from his saddle.

"Quick, Emma, get a light out here!" He ran over to Sam as Emma brought a lantern.

"Get away from me. I ain't dead." Sam opened his eyes as Ryan began probing him for bullet holes.

"You've got a slug in your leg," Ryan said.

"I'm all right."

"Sure you are. You fell off your horse, didn't you?"

"I was took by surprise," Sam muttered. "I looked down an' there was all that blood." He looked embarrassed.

"Well, that slug's gotta come out," Ryan said. "But I want you where I can stick you in a bed afterward, and Monty's got enough on his hands here. Can you ride?"

"I can ride," Sam said. He knew that if those gunmen came back, he would be in the way. Gritting his teeth, he sat up.

"Good," Ryan said. He tied his bandanna around Sam's leg. He was worried, but he hid it from Sam. "Pony, I want you and Bill to stay here tonight. Julio"—he looked at the fourth cowhand—"you get to the other homesteaders' places. Tell 'em to keep a sharp lookout. I don't think those toughs will make trouble anyplace else—one of them's wounded, and anyway they were after Monty—but I'm not taking any chances. Tomorrow I'm gonna blast Hank Purchase and give him something to worry about."

"What about him?" Pony Simkins jerked a thumb at the body slumped over the watering trough.

"Take him out somewhere and dump him," Ryan said shortly. "If we're lucky, the critters'll get to him. I wouldn't want Hank to have to worry about a shooting," he added sarcastically.

They lifted Sam Harkness into his saddle, and Emma came and stood beside Ryan's horse. "Thank you for what you done," she said. "I reckon Monty and me are lucky we got friends."

Ryan brushed her cheek lightly with his fingers. "Anybody's lucky when they have friends," he said gently. "Me included. You go back in the house now and try not to worry. Pony and Bill will be here."

He swung into his own saddle, reached down to take hold of the reins of Sam's horse, and rode off, setting as fast a pace as he thought Sam could stand.

"Leggo of those," Sam protested. "I ain't a baby."

"Just shut up and hang on."

It was a lot longer ride at a fast walk than it had been at a gallop. Soon Sam stopped protesting that he could hold his own reins and started hanging onto the saddle, his head dropping low on his chest. Ryan stopped and looked at the bandage once and tightened it, while Sam murmured something unintelligible. Ryan mounted up again and rode on, grim-faced.

When they got to the Broken R, there was a lamp still burning downstairs. Ryan left Sam in the saddle and banged on the door to roust whoever was still awake to come and help him. As he half expected, it was Elizabeth Bradley.

When she opened the door and saw Sam slumped in the saddle, she flew down the steps after Tim Ryan. "What happened?"

"He's got a bullet in his leg. It's got to come out before it starts to fester, and we don't have the time for me to ride into Shawnee and bring back the doctor. Old Wallace is about half drunk most of the time anyway."

"All right." Elizabeth helped him get Sam down off the horse. When they had Sam slung over Ryan's shoulder, she went ahead to open the door for him. "Put him on my bed," she said briskly. "It's closest."

Ryan, who had been about to inform her that he was going to do just that, blinked at her matter-of-fact tone but did not comment. "I need hot water and some clean rags," he said, but Elizabeth had already gone. As he laid Sam gently onto the bed, he heard the oven's fire door open and close in the kitchen. When he came in, she was dropping a thin, dull knife and a pair of pliers into a wash pan beside the big kettle. Then she took a clean bed sheet and a pair of scissors and went back into the bedroom.

Ryan followed her in and watched as she snipped the edge of the sheet and began tearing it into strips. Sam tossed his head restlessly on the pillow. In the light of the tin lamp, his cheeks were ashen. Ryan pulled Sam's boots off, took the scissors from Elizabeth, and carefully cut the trouser leg away from the wound. He unbuckled Sam's belt and unbuttoned the trousers, and together they eased them carefully down over his hips.

"Better to do it now while he's unconscious," Elizabeth said, as Ryan looked worriedly at Sam's chalky face. The kettle began to sing in the kitchen, and she went out again and came back with a basin and the kettle. In the pocket of her apron she had a cake of soap and the freshly washed knife and pliers. She spread them out on a towel on the washstand and looked doubtfully at Tim Ryan. "Have you ever taken a bullet out before?"

"Yeah," Ryan said.

"Thank goodness," Elizabeth said with relief. "Because I haven't."

"You've watched, though," Ryan said. He gestured at the things he would need, neatly arrayed on the washstand.

"I've watched worse than this," Elizabeth said. Her eyes clouded. "I've watched them take a man's leg off, when there was no morphine to be had." She looked at Sam and sighed. "It's bad enough in a war. How did this happen?"

"War," Ryan said. "Of a sort. Your friend Bigelow hired some guns to try to burn Monty Lang's house down!"

"Oh, no." Elizabeth looked at him with horror. "Emma—"

"Emma's all right. But one of Bigelow's hired guns was killed, and another one wounded—and you just forget I told you anything about it."

Elizabeth stared at him. Two men shot and another one killed, and all over a fight about rangeland. "Are you sure it was Mr. Bigelow?" she whispered.

"I can't prove it," Ryan said. He washed his hands in

her basin with the soap, while she looked at him miserably. Then he picked up the knife. "You clean the wound
for me," he said. "Your hands are neater than mine."

Elizabeth nodded, feeling numb. She took a rag, dipped
it in the hot water, and wiped Sam's leg, her small fingers
cleaning gently around the edges of the wound. The skin
was dark with coagulated blood and fragments of his trousers. It was bleeding only slightly, but she had seen men
die of less serious wounds than this because of infection.

"I can't believe Mr. Bigelow would . . ." She stopped.

"You know damn well he would!" Ryan snapped. "If you
weren't so stubborn, you'd admit it. I told you what he
was like."

"You never told me anything!"

"I told you to stay away from him." Ryan picked up the
knife and began to probe carefully in the wound.

Elizabeth held the lamp close above his hands. "You
never told me why you wanted me to stay away from
him," she whispered. "Lily Cummings told me—"

Ryan's eyes snapped up. "What did Lily Cummings tell
you?"

"That you fight with him over the homesteaders."

Ryan concentrated on the bullet again.

"If she had thought Mr. Bigelow would do anything like
this, I know she would have told me," Elizabeth said.
"You can't be sure."

"I'm sure," Ryan said. "If it hadn't been for Bigelow's
standing orders, his men would never have lynched those
three cow thieves. You're just too damn green to see
what's in front of your face."

Elizabeth gave him an outraged look. "This is a horrible
country," she said.

"Hold the lamp over here some more," Ryan said.

Sam twitched violently and groaned as Ryan probed
with the knife.

"Give him some whiskey if he wakes up enough to
swallow it," Ryan said.

"Whiskey's a poor anesthetic," Elizabeth said. "Have
you any laudanum?"

"No," Ryan said shortly. "My wife used to take it for
sick headaches. I threw it out."

"That was wasteful of you, Mr. Ryan," Elizabeth said. "It would be helpful now to have it."

Sam's eyes fluttered open. "I'll take the whiskey," he said. "Ryan, you got hands like a cow."

"At least I'm sober," Ryan said. But he left the wound alone while Elizabeth went to get the whiskey bottle.

Sam raised his head and swallowed as much as he could, then dropped back on the pillow wearily. "You can be sober," he muttered. "I don't wanna be."

"You hang on," Ryan said. "I've nearly got it."

Elizabeth held the lamp with one hand and reached out to Sam with the other. He gripped it, squeezing hard as Tim Ryan probed as gently as he could. After a moment, Ryan said, "I got it. Hold this, just like I got it." Elizabeth released her hand from Sam's grip and held the little knife steady. Ryan slid the narrow-nosed pliers into the wound.

"Damn!" Sam yelped and lurched as Ryan pulled the bullet out. He showed it to Sam and then put it on the towel. Sam's eyelids fluttered.

Ryan waited until his patient's eyes were closed completely and then poured a good dollop of whiskey into the wound. Sam recoiled from the searing alcohol, cursing him.

"Go get something to make a dressing while he calms down," Ryan told Elizabeth.

Elizabeth nodded, a slight smile forming. Since Sam was able to get that angry, he would be all right. She went upstairs to ransack the linen chest for an old, clean towel.

Sam slowly began to relax as the pain lessened, and he stopped raving at Ryan. "Why didn't you warn me you were gonna do that?" he said finally.

"I figured you'd rather not know ahead of time."

"Oh. Damn." Sam propped himself up a little on his elbows. "I've known fifty-year-old whores with a lighter touch than you got," he said balefully. He looked down at himself and discovered another source of complaint. "You mean I been lyin' here in my underdrawers in front of Mrs. Bradley?"

"You're lucky that bullet wasn't a bit higher, or you'd have been lying there with a damn sight less than that,"

Ryan said. "She was a nurse. I figured she could stand the sight. See that you tone down your language a little before she gets back, though," he added.

Elizabeth came back with an old cotton towel, worn to a linty softness. "Did you clean it?" she asked Ryan.

"Yeah," Sam said. "You just bandage it up. I reckon I can get out to the bunkhouse."

"You will sleep here," Elizabeth told him firmly. "I'll sleep with Charlie."

"I can't put you outta your room," Sam protested.

"I want you where I can keep an eye on that leg," Elizabeth said. "So don't argue." She put a dressing on the wound and bandaged it with practiced fingers. She had also found one of Tim Ryan's nightshirts, and she made Sam sit up while she unbuttoned his shirt and put it on him. "Now you go to sleep. I'll look at that leg again in the morning. It's got to be kept clean, and you're to stay off it."

"Yes, Mama," Sam murmured.

Elizabeth grinned at him and blew out the lamp. Ryan picked up the basin and the bloody knife and pliers and followed her out the door.

"That's a nice boy," Elizabeth said. "He deserves better than what happened to him tonight."

"So do you," Ryan said. "I'm sorry I got sore at you about George Bigelow."

"You made your point," Elizabeth said. "If you are right about Mr. Bigelow, there can be no question of my having anything more to do with him." Her face, in the smoky shadows of the kitchen, looked depressed.

"Cheer up," Ryan said. "There's always Angus. You can develop quite a taste for bagpipes, if you work at it."

Elizabeth glared at him.

"Sorry," Ryan said quickly. "I just meant there're more men around here than George Bigelow. You ought to get married. You'd make someone a good wife. I take back what I said about being green. At least you didn't faint in there." He jerked his thumb in the direction of the bedroom.

"I told you, I've seen worse than that," Elizabeth said. "And I don't faint, anyway."

"No, I see that you don't," Ryan mumbled. "It's just that Caroline would have. Or said she was going to." He turned away and started wiping the blood from the pliers.

Elizabeth thought she heard both anger and embarrassment in his voice. What had Caroline Ryan really been like? But she knew better than to pursue it. She looked at his back helplessly. This was probably not an opportune time to tell him that George Bigelow was supposed to take her to church tomorrow.

Chapter Eight

Elizabeth knotted the sash of her wrapper and tiptoed from Charlie's bedroom into her own. She was hoping not to wake Sam, but his eyes were already open, and he gave her a cheerful smile.

"Good morning. How are you feeling?" she asked him.

"I've felt better," he said. "But pretty good, considering."

Elizabeth felt his forehead. "Good. No fever. I'll change that dressing when we get back from church." She glanced out the bedroom window. She had decided to tell Bigelow that she would not go to church with him, although she firmly believed that Bigelow had nothing to do with the shooting at the Langs' last night.

"You reckon Mrs. Cummings will be there?" Sam asked.

"She always is," Elizabeth said. She remembered Sam's interest in Lily's Swedish bound girl. "And Inga, too, I expect. Shall I take her a message?"

Sam looked embarrassed. "Well, you might just give her my regards," he murmured. "Tell her I ain't dead."

"I'll do that." Elizabeth whisked her Sunday clothes from the wardrobe and scuttled into Charlie's room. She prodded her son out of bed and sent him to the privy while she dressed.

"Why are you dressing in here?" Charlie wanted to know when he returned.

"I slept in here," Elizabeth said, "only you were too deeply asleep to notice."

"Why?"

"Because Sam is in my room. He got hurt last night, and we put him to bed there."

"Hurt? How?" Charlie, putting his stockings on, paused on one foot to learn the details.

Elizabeth sighed. "He was shot while helping Mr. Ryan defend Mr. Lang's homestead against some hired gunmen. It was dreadful," she said firmly as Charlie's eyes lit up with curiosity, "but he is going to be all right."

"Shot?" Charlie hopped on the other foot, hurrying into his stockings. "Can I see the bullet hole?"

"You can help me change the dressing when we get back," she said. "Now get your shirt and knickers on."

"Yes, ma'am! Are you gonna let the girls help?"

Elizabeth thought about that. Carrie and Susannah should learn that caring for the sick was something a lady knew how to do. After her conversation with their father last night, she thought he would approve. The children all liked Sam, so she would have to set visiting hours, as well, or they would wear him out.

When she was dressed, she went into the dining room to supervise the children's meal. Tim Ryan and his cowhands were already at the table for Sunday breakfast. Ryan was in his work clothes; after his first appearance in church, he had not gone again.

"I looked in on Sam," Elizabeth told him. "He's doing fine."

"I reckon he just likes the bed he's in," Cal Hodges said with an unpleasant leer.

Elizabeth pursed her lips and ignored him. "There's no sign of fever," she told Ryan, nibbling a biscuit.

"You let me know when he's strong enough to move out to the bunkhouse," Ryan said. "I don't want to put you out any longer than we have to."

"And you keep your mouth shut," she heard Pony Simkins saying under his breath to Cal. "You weren't out there gettin' shot at. You got no call to be runnin' your mouth off now."

Simkins and Bill Ennis had ridden in at dawn to say there had been no more trouble at the Langs', and Julio Reyes had reported that the hired guns had headed south.

Sheriff Henry Purchase, a tall, bland-looking man whom Elizabeth had met once, was due back in town this afternoon, and Elizabeth knew that Tim Ryan was planning to be in his office waiting for him.

The rattle of buggy wheels in the yard caught her ear, and Elizabeth looked out in time to see George Bigelow's surrey pull up to the porch. "Excuse me," she murmured, rising. She hurried to meet him before Ryan came out and started a fight. She could not believe that Bigelow would threaten the Langs with hired guns, whatever he thought of homesteaders.

"George," she said, tripping down the steps with her hand outstretched and a gracious smile on her face.

"Mrs. Bradley, you're a vision." George Bigelow smiled and started to step down from the surrey. "Did you just call me 'George'?"

"It was an oversight," Elizabeth said. "Mr. Bigelow, I am very sorry, but I simply can't drive to church with you this morning." She hesitated. "There was some trouble at Monty Lang's place last night, and I'm afraid Mr. Ryan holds you responsible. With the frame of mind he's in, I think I had better keep the peace until he sees reason."

Bigelow's smile became bland and a little smug. Surely Elizabeth Bradley would not risk losing George Bigelow as a suitor by siding with Tim Ryan.

"I wouldn't make you uncomfortable for the world," he said. "But don't you worry. Ryan'll come round. The whole thing was his fault, anyway. All we wanted to do was put a little fear into those cow thieves, keep them from rustling my herd. Nobody would have been hurt if Ryan hadn't stuck his nose in."

Elizabeth stared at him aghast. He had done it! He was sitting there in that surrey admitting it, and expecting her to go along with him. Several furious sentences came into her mind, and she was selecting the best one when Tim Ryan came down the porch steps in a towering rage.

"Bigelow, get the hell off my land before I shoot you!" he yelled. He pointed a finger at Elizabeth. "And you— you get in the house!"

Elizabeth was outraged, beside herself with anger at them both. How dare George Bigelow come here this morning! How dare Tim Ryan treat her like an errant schoolgirl without enough sense to make her own judgments! With her last shred of self-control she realized that anything she said would fan the fury. Tim Ryan looked capable of anything now. She turned and marched into the house.

Behind her, she heard George Bigelow say bitingly to Ryan, "You keep going this way, you'll get in as much trouble as your friend Lang." The buggy whip cracked, and the surrey rattled out of the yard.

I've been a fool, Elizabeth thought. *Tim Ryan has been right about George Bigelow all along*. She clenched her fists. She would not apologize. Tim Ryan should not have treated her that way.

Out in the yard, Ryan grimly watched as Bigelow's surrey drove out of sight. He watched the dust cloud that followed it with an urge to murder. He heard the door bang behind him and turned to find Elizabeth on the porch with the children. She had her prayer book and a parasol under one arm, and was pulling on her gloves.

"Where the hell do you think you're going?" Ryan demanded.

Elizabeth gave him a frozen look. "To church. In the buggy. Surely that's not forbidden?"

She marched past him, gathering the children around her skirts like a flock of chicks in the presence of a wolf. Ryan watched her go in silence.

> Shall we gather by the river,
> The beautiful, beautiful river
> That flows by the throne of God.

Elizabeth's teeth were still chattering as she sang. She felt a perfectly unholy desire that Tim Ryan should be gathered to his fathers. She had never been so angry at anyone.

"You look fit to be tied," Lily observed as they came out of the church into the bright Wyoming sun.

Elizabeth paused long enough to shake Mr. Leslie's hand and compliment him on the sermon, which she had not heard. "I am," she said to Lily when they were out of earshot. "If the Lord really wanted to oblige me, he would have the entire male sex removed to the North Pole."

"Heavens," Lily said. She looked at Elizabeth suspiciously. "What happened last night? There are the most amazing rumors all over town. Is that what's bothering you this morning?"

Elizabeth gave Lily a succinct account of the evening's and morning's events. "I don't ever want to see George Bigelow again. Nobody's ever going to be able to prove anything, and he knows it. I suspect he thinks that's amusing, which just makes him more reprehensible in my book. This is the most dreadful country! How can things like this happen?" Her voice rose, and she realized that people were looking at her with interest. She lowered it hastily. "And as for Timothy Ryan, I'd just as soon shoot him as look at him right now. How could he even think that I'd do anything but send George Bigelow away? He absolutely humiliated me!"

Lily wore a worried expression, and she appeared to come to some decision. "You come along home and have dinner with Robert and me. Inga's been in a swivet all morning, ever since she heard the rumors that are going around. Her nerves made her too ill to attend church, she said. She's convinced Sam's dead or in jail or heaven only knows what. I have never seen her so upset. I think she's really serious about him." Lily sighed. "I suppose I'll have to write off her contract and let her get married before her bound time is up. She'll never last another two years after this. Oh, well, we'll have a wedding, and it will be fun. This makes the third," she added.

"Third?"

"The third bound girl," Lily said. "Some people will make them work out their time no matter what, but I haven't the heart. Inga's the third one to get married. Their passage doesn't cost that much, and I think their contracts are indecently long anyway."

"I take it other employers don't feel that way," Elizabeth said, distracted from her irritation with Tim Ryan.

"No, and some people are just dreadful and work them to death. But most of the bound servants stick it out. Inga and her sister didn't have much in the way of prospects at home in Sweden. Anyone with the gumption to cross the Atlantic and work until they've paid off their passage has got what it takes to make it out here. Let's collect the children and go have dinner. I notice George Bigelow didn't show his face in church this morning," she said.

Elizabeth, now that she had vented her anger, was beginning to feel a little better. She put the children in the buggy and followed the Cummings's buggy down the street into town.

Inga was at the door of the Cummings house when they drove up. Elizabeth reassured her about Sam's recovery and received a stammered and tearful thanks.

They sat down to Sunday dinner. Carrie and Susannah displayed their recently acquired company manners in a fashion that Lily said did them credit. As soon as they had eaten their pie, however, she sent them out into the yard to play with Charlie and her own three.

"And now," she said, "we are going to go into the parlor where we can be comfortable." She turned to her husband with a determined look. "Robert, I'm going to tell her."

"Lily—"

"My mind is made up," Lily said. "And if you don't want to be a party to it, you can just go off somewhere, and then you'll have a clear conscience."

"You have a mighty convenient opinion of what it takes to keep a conscience clear," Robert said. "I made a promise to Tim, and so did you."

Elizabeth was beginning to feel uncomfortable and very curious. "If it's something private to do with Mr. Ryan . . ." she began.

"It's something you are going to have to know if you are going to go on working for him," Lily said. "And particularly if George Bigelow is courting you seriously."

"He may be serious," Elizabeth said indignantly, "but I wouldn't have him now if . . . someone were giving him away. I would have told him so this morning if Mr. Ryan hadn't decided to make it his business to do so."

"There, Robert, you see?" Lily said. She stood, gathering up her tan satin skirts. "Elizabeth, you come with me. Robert, you can stay or go as you please."

"I'm coming," Robert said. "Maybe you're right. I'd like to go shoot Bigelow myself. He's been after me for months to find a legal way to steal Monty Lang's land. It seems he finally decided to believe me when I told him I couldn't and wouldn't, and to take matters into his own hands."

Elizabeth followed them nervously into the parlor. She had an overpowering desire to know about Tim Ryan, but with all this talk of secrets and promises, she was certain that whatever Lily would tell her was something he did not want her to know. As soon as Lily spoke, she was sure of it.

"Well," Lily said, "it was Caroline." She looked at the framed wedding photograph of herself and Robert that stood on the parlor table. As newlyweds, even in the motionless pose required for photography, they looked young, excited, a little silly—plainly in love with each other. "Poor Tim," Lily said. "He always envied us. We've always been so happy together." She gave her husband an affectionate grin. "Despite certain disagreements. Tim wanted a marriage like that so desperately, and what he got was Caroline, who was the most self-centered woman ever put on the face of the earth."

"Anyone in Shawnee who thinks they know what they're talking about will tell you Tim never remarried because he's still mourning her," Robert said. "In a way, it's true."

"Caroline didn't want Tim," Lily explained. "She wanted his ranch. She wanted ease. She thought it was going to be like the plantation her parents lost in the war, all green lawns, and pretty fields, and servants, and parties. When she got here . . . There was nothing but mud, a sod house, and a herd of longhorns that scared her to death, and all this open space with not a soul to talk to but Tim and his cowhands, who were gone most of the time. We tried to make her welcome—Shawnee does have an occasional social life—but it wasn't what she'd expected. And then she had the twins, and they tied her down even more. I don't think Caroline had any idea how much trouble children are, especially two at once. She had always had a nurse when she was little."

"So did I," Elizabeth said. "Darling old Susie. I adored her. More than Mama, really; I spent more time with

Susie. But I thought, when I was old enough to think about children, that I wanted my children to love me the way I'd loved Susie. I wasn't going to let a nurse take over." She sighed ruefully. "Of course, by the time I had Charlie, we couldn't have afforded a nurse if I'd wanted one."

"Caroline didn't see it that way, I'm afraid," Lily said. "Tim adored those girls from the moment they were born, but Caroline just started to feel frantic and discontented. Every year she was out here it got worse. They were miserable, Tim and Caroline, I mean. Caroline wanting things they couldn't afford, things that just weren't possible on the frontier, and Tim tried to give them to her. He built that house for her, bought her that piano. He borrowed the money from us to pay for the piano until he got the profits from that year's cattle drive. I think it must have taken nearly all he got to pay us back. The girls were about three then."

"That must have been just before she died," Elizabeth said.

"She didn't die," Lily said flatly. "She left him. She ran away with a man who promised to take her to San Francisco and give her the life she wanted. I doubt that he did. The man was a born liar, but I've never been able to feel sorry for her, not after what she did to Tim."

Elizabeth stared at her. "But they buried her. Elvina Fishburn told me she was at the funeral."

"They buried a coffin with a hundred pounds of bricks," Lily said. "Tim couldn't bear to have his girls grow up knowing that their mother had left them. There were some cases of cholera that year. He told everyone that she had caught it and died suddenly. He filled that coffin with bricks and buried it. There weren't that many people out here then, no doctors to sign death certificates, and his only ranch hands were the boys he hired by the season for the trail drive. Mr. Leslie hadn't come yet either. Tim hired a traveling preacher to say the service over those bricks. We were the only people who knew about it, although Tim told me later that he got drunk one night and told that Meg Callahan." Lily made a face. "I suppose I shouldn't blame him; he had to go somewhere for comfort. I will say this for her: She's never told a soul, so far as I know."

"Then he's still married," Elizabeth said, with a cold, sinking feeling.

Lily shook her head. "No. Robert got him a very quiet divorce a year later, on grounds of desertion. I don't think Tim had any intention of marrying again. He just wanted to erase Caroline from his life."

"Poor man," Elizabeth said quietly. "What made you decide to tell me? What has this got to do with George Bigelow?"

"The man she ran off with was Bigelow's foreman," Robert said. "Bigelow told everyone he had fired the man, but Tim's always suspected that George knew Caroline had gone with him. He's afraid Bigelow may spill the story out of sheer spite, and then Carrie and Susannah will find out. Tim loves those girls. Except for their coloring, they're the image of Caroline, and they're everything he'd hoped his wife would be and wasn't."

"That's the other reason we told you," Lily said. "You look like Caroline, too. Oh, not identical, but the same build and coloring, the same type of face. You and Caroline have the same background. His sister Mattie doesn't know about Caroline. Mattie thinks she died, and I suspect she thought she'd found Tim the perfect second wife when she sent you out here."

"Oh, no." Elizabeth put her face in her hands.

"So you can see why Tim gets a little crazy at the idea of your taking up with George Bigelow. It isn't just that Tim and George oppose each other over the homesteaders. It may not be rational, but it's understandable when you know about Caroline."

Elizabeth bit her lip. "Well, he'll just have to get used to the idea that I'm not a ghost. He may not need a wife, but he does need a housekeeper, and since I have no intention of being anything else, maybe we can get along." She stood up. "Thank you for telling me. Now I'd better take the children home."

When she had gone, Lily looked at Robert. "What do you think?" she asked.

"God knows," Robert said.

*   *   *

Elizabeth returned to the Broken R with the children just in time for supper and found a subdued Tim Ryan wearing a baleful look. He seemed as if he had spent the day doing some careful thinking. He was cordial, if a little restrained, at supper. He glared so fiercely at Cal Hodges when Cal asked that Elizabeth "pass the biscuits" that Cal was silent for the rest of the meal.

After supper, Elizabeth sat down at the piano. She left her bedroom door open so that Sam could hear the singing. When she told the children that it was their bedtime, the cowboys got up to go to the bunkhouse, tipping their hats to her and calling cheerful jokes to Sam. Ryan did not move. He just sat in the parlor, looking at the silent piano. When Elizabeth came downstairs after putting the girls to bed, he was still there. She tucked Charlie in, looked in on Sam for a moment, and came back to the parlor to find Ryan still sitting there. She stood in the doorway, hesitating.

"Will you blow out the lamp or shall I?" she asked him.

"I'll do it," he said. "I feel uneasy tonight. Not much like sleeping."

I've got to get on a better footing with him, Elizabeth thought. *This is horrible.* She came in quietly and sat down in a chair. He did not move. "Did you have any luck with the sheriff today?" she asked quietly.

Ryan snorted. "I got a lot of big talk that isn't going to amount to any action. About what I expected. But he'll think twice about leaving town when he knows there's trouble coming. I pinned his ears back pretty good."

"Then he can't do anything about what happened last night?"

"Can't. Won't."

His tense face looked sad in the rosy glow of the lamp. He sat on one end of the dark green velvet settee, not as if he were resting but as if he were too cold or too tired to move. His eyes were the only mobile thing about him. They rested on her face darkly.

"You doing all right?" he said. "I reckon what happened this morning might've really upset you. If it did, I'm sorry."

"Don't be," Elizabeth said. "I don't know whether I

actually would have married Mr. Bigelow or not. Assuming that he was going to ask me." But they both knew that Bigelow would have. "But I would rather find out that it was a mistake now. To find out afterward . . ." Her voice trailed away. "I did that once. . . ."

"Yeah, that's the worst," Ryan said. "Finding out afterward."

I can't let this go on, Elizabeth thought. *He's got to know that Lily told me.* She walked across the gleaming floor and sat down again on the other end of the settee. "I must tell you," she said quietly. "I visited Lily Cummings after church this morning. She told me about your wife."

"Goddamn her to hell," Ryan said. It was almost a whisper.

"Don't," Elizabeth said. "I had to know about it if I'm going to go on working here. Not just because of George Bigelow, but because of the girls. They must never know about it; you were right. I can't protect them if I don't know what to protect them from. Please, don't hate Lily. If she didn't care about you, she wouldn't have told me."

The stiffness eased from Ryan's body, and his tense, rigid frame relaxed wearily. She sensed that he was relieved that Lily had told her what he had been unable to share himself.

"She was so beautiful," he said sadly.

"I can see that," Elizabeth said. "In the girls."

His eyes brooded darkly at her in the dim light. "They're about all I've got," he said. "Two good things that somehow came out of misery."

They sat in silence for a moment.

"If you're feeling sorry for me—" Ryan said.

"No," Elizabeth said gently. "Oh, no. I think I was just feeling like a fool. I always thought I was the only one who had that particular cross to bear. You see, I knew six months after I married Charles that I shouldn't have done it. Odd, how we always think we're alone." She brushed a hand across her eyes.

Ryan looked at her intently. "You don't have to tell me if you don't want to," he said. "Not just to make things even."

"No," Elizabeth said. "It's almost a relief to tell someone. You see, I couldn't ever tell anybody at home. I was too proud for that."

"Pride's a pretty painful virtue," Ryan said.

"It's a very lonely one," Elizabeth said. "But there was Charlie, too. I didn't want him ever to know. He loved his father. Children should be able to love their parents without reservations."

"Yeah, I guess it's about all we can give 'em."

"And, you know, there weren't very many men to marry. The war took them all. All the poor boys . . ." Elizabeth found herself crying, for anything and everything: for the boys dead in the war; for Charles, who had probably made a mistake, too, when he married her; maybe even for Tim Ryan. She was not sure, but the tears seemed to flow of their own accord.

"Here, now, don't cry," Ryan said. He got up and took a decanter and a glass from the cupboard in his office across the hall. He poured a stiff drink and swallowed it quickly before he returned to the parlor, splashed a dollop of whiskey in the glass, and handed it to her. "Here, now, drink this. You've had a tough day. My granny used to say there was a lot of ease in a shot of whiskey," he said as she protested.

As Elizabeth drank, the whiskey scalded her mouth and throat, but after a moment she found the tears stopped streaming down her cheeks. "We were all so young and stupid," she whispered desolately. She lifted wet eyes to his and found his cat-green gaze studying her with a look that was not pity but some innate understanding.

The whiskey seemed to soak into her body, easing not just the tears, but somehow the sorrow behind them as well. Or maybe that was Tim Ryan's arm around her, and the soft thud of his heart under her cheek as he stroked her hair with comforting hands.

"I'm stupid, too," he said into her hair.

She leaned against his chest and heard his heartbeat grow stronger, faster. His lips brushed her forehead. All the desperate times that she had let Charles hold her like this flooded through her mind and were gone. Never, in all their marriage, had her body responded to Charles as it now yearned for Tim Ryan. She lifted her eyes to his and saw the hunger in his green gaze.

Ryan's arm tightened about her, and suddenly his mouth came down on hers. Desire flooded over her, and she swam somewhere just under the surface, letting it come.

He picked her up in his arms and bent to blow out the parlor lamp. As he started up the stairs, she wrapped her arms around his neck.

He set her on her feet in the darkened bedroom, and his fingers slipped open the buttons down the back of her dress. They moved in silence to the soft tick of the clock and the shrill yelp of a prairie wolf somewhere in the distance. The dress slid from her shoulders. Moonlight slanted through the window, setting his face into high relief, the sharp plane of cheekbones, the black, winging brows, the thin, mobile line of his mouth as he bent his face toward hers. The fallen dress was a puddle of black and silver at her feet.

He kissed her. She swayed toward him, felt his hands unhook the front of her corset, and let it fall with her dress. He pressed his hands against her breasts, bare beneath the thin cotton chemise. The moonlight was dizzying, dark and light, a fleeting pattern like a magic lantern, hurrying, sweeping them both into its spell.

Tim Ryan pulled away from her suddenly, his eyes still on hers, and began to unbuckle his belt. Elizabeth steadied herself against the brass footrail of the bed and unlaced her shoes. Ryan knelt at her feet and pulled them off for her. His hands were trembling now as they reached up under her petticoat to draw off her stockings and then slowly untie the drawstring at her waist. Her pantalettes slid to the floor.

His face, when he stood up, was hungry and hesitant, as if he were afraid that she might tell him to stop. Elizabeth drew him toward her, unbuttoning his shirt, and he made a low, soft sigh of relief. He bent to pull off his boots and trousers, and she eased him down to her on the bed.

Tim Ryan lay beside Elizabeth Bradley, his breath still coming in ragged gasps, his hair damp with sweat. The moonlight glowed silvery on the bare line of her hips. Her hair was a silver tangle in the bedclothes. She looked at him with a faint, sleepy smile, seeming not to mind that he was still looking at her now, afterward. Caroline, he thought, with a faint return of the old brutal bitterness, had never let him even undress her. She had always been in bed, her nightgown tied under her chin, before she even let him in the room. Now he could not remember what she had looked like naked. Maybe she had looked like Elizabeth. He did not know.

Elizabeth stirred, and he caught such a look of longing in her moon-washed eyes that he forgot Caroline. His heart began to hammer in his chest, and he bent over her again, still hungry.

Chapter Nine

Elizabeth awoke by some sixth sense a half hour before the rest of the household began to stir. Seeing in the half-light of beginning dawn not Charlie but Tim Ryan beside her in the unfamiliar bed, it was all she could do not to groan aloud. Her temples throbbed from the whiskey. It had looked like such a little whiskey in the glass, but she had never drunk any before. She wondered if it made everyone feel like this in the morning, and if it did, why they drank it. She remembered the floating, euphoric feeling it had given her. Had that been the whiskey, or Tim Ryan?

He was still asleep, his tanned face turned toward hers on the pillow, unaccountably young looking under the dark tangle of hair and the dark sweep of closed lashes; the usual sardonic look had vanished in slumber. *Why did I do it?* she thought. But she knew, bitterly enough, why she had done it. No amount of justifying it would explain away the cold, simple fact that she loved him, that she had been fighting against loving him for weeks.

What if Little Deer or the children see me here? The thought jolted her to reality. She rolled out of bed and scrambled on the floor for her scattered underthings.

The movement woke Ryan. He opened his eyes and looked at her as if he, too, were momentarily startled.

"I must have been crazy," Elizabeth muttered. She snatched up her petticoat and held it in front of her.

"I reckon we both were," Ryan said. He propped himself up on his elbows. His head ached. He could not blame that on the single shot of whiskey he had when he brought Elizabeth hers. Brooding over his righteous indignation at George Bigelow and the quarrel he had had earlier in the morning with Elizabeth, he had downed three or four drinks while she had been putting the children to bed. "I also reckon I ought to send for the preacher," he added.

"Certainly not," Elizabeth said, still holding her petticoat in front of her. "I'm not going to be married because someone feels that he ought to."

"Women have got married for a lot less," Ryan said, too rattled by his sudden realization of responsibility to be diplomatic. "Girls have had to get married because a buggy axle broke and they had to stay out all night with a boy."

"That's because they got caught," Elizabeth said.

"You mean it's all right if you don't get caught?" Ryan inquired.

"Not exactly . . . No, of course I don't." She waited for him to look politely away so she could get dressed, but he kept watching. She gave up waiting and began to pull her drawers on with the petticoat tucked under her chin. She doubted that it was hiding much. "I just meant that I'm not a girl anymore," she said testily, "and I can take care of myself."

"You sure as hell aren't an old lady," Ryan said. "And you aren't one of those girls at Meg's place. If this gets out, they'll run you outta town. I can't let that happen for something that was my fault."

"It was just as much my fault as yours," Elizabeth said. "So you'll have to come up with a better reason for marriage than what happened last night." He did not look as if he was going to. "Now, if you will excuse me . . ." She turned her back to put on her chemise and corset. That done, she picked up her stockings and petticoat and dressed in silence. Her dress, however, buttoned up the back. After watching her struggle with it, Ryan pulled on his drawers and got out of bed to help her.

"Thank you." She refused to look at him.

"You better brush your hair," he commented.

She looked at herself in the mirror over the marble-topped dresser. Her pale hair hung rakishly over one shoulder, and she looked wild-eyed. The hairpins had all fallen out somewhere in Tim Ryan's bed. She shook out the sheets and pillowcases, searching for them without comment, unable to think of any appropriate remark, although several horribly inappropriate ones came rather readily to mind. Ryan handed her his own hairbrush, and she pinned her hair up hastily and fled.

He watched her go with the old sardonic look back on his face. Well, he had offered, and she had turned him down. He wondered why she had climbed in bed with him. It must have been the loneliness and whiskey, he supposed. Or perhaps she had someone else in mind, he thought, sourly.

Surely she would not marry Bigelow now. She had said as much. Maybe it was Angus Ogilvie. Well, he hoped she got good and sick of bagpipe music.

Ryan started to dress, cursing under his breath. He had no intention of marrying again, but when he had posed the suggestion, out of propriety, it had sounded pretty good. He had been stung when she refused.

Breakfast was strained. Two almost-palpable clouds of tension hung over Mr. Ryan and Mrs. Bradley, who had been Tim and Elizabeth the night before and who had now, hastily and self-consciously, reverted to formality. The others at the table seemed not to notice. The children chattered cheerfully, devising reasons (none of them acceptable) why they should not go to school this morning. Little Deer slung plates on the table and snatched them off again as soon as they were empty; she had things to do. The cowboys ate with the efficiency of an engine stoking up. And Sam Harkness bellowed from Elizabeth's room that if Mrs. Bradley would not let him get out of bed, he was going to come to the table anyway in his underdrawers. Only Cal Hodges, with the instinctive inquisitiveness of a ferret, looked thoughtfully at the boss of the Broken R and at his housekeeper. *He thinks he knows something,*

Ryan decided, and tried to look less surly. Unsure of whether he had succeeded, he gave Cal a look that indicated that whatever Cal thought he knew, he had better not voice it.

"There's a town meeting tonight," Ryan said as he pushed back his chair and stood up, "about the range thieving that's been going on. Anyone who has something to say is welcome." He glanced at Elizabeth, including her in the invitation. "You too, Mrs. Bradley. It might tone them down some to have the ladies there."

"Thank you," Elizabeth said gravely. "I shall be glad to be a restraining influence."

"What's a restraining influence?" Susannah asked.

"Someone that keeps 'em from cussing too much," Pony Simkins told her.

Ryan sighed. "I'd settle for something to keep them from shooting each other," he said. "Feelings are running pretty high about what happened at Monty Lang's place. I thought a town meeting was better than a town gunfight."

"You set it up?" Pony Simkins said. "Bigelow'll love that."

"Anyone on the council's got a right to call a meeting," Ryan answered. The town council was composed of Tim Ryan, George Bigelow, Angus Ogilvie, Clyde Sawyer, Joe Fishburn, and the Rev. Mr. William Leslie, serving as the voice of peace and brotherhood. As things stood, peace and brotherhood generally got shouted down. "I browbeat Sheriff Purchase into saying he'd be there," Ryan added. "For what he's worth."

Pony Simkins snorted. "He ain't worth much. Town council'd do better to hire themselves a sheriff that can't be bought so cheap. Old Hank's got a name on him to fit his character."

"Shawnee's been through three sheriffs in the last four years," Ryan said. "The one before Hank took off on the next stage after the town council got in a fistfight while they were showing him his office. You want the job, I'll put in your application."

"Not me," Pony said. "My gunslingin' days ended back when I was young and stupid. Besides, I ain't got the clout. You oughtta hire on yourself."

"I got a ranch to run," Ryan said. "And I'm not exactly popular right now. Mrs. Bradley, if you want to come, you'll need to be ready at six."

"Can we go?" Carrie asked.

"No," Ryan and Elizabeth answered together.

"That's not fair!"

"It doesn't have to be fair," Ryan said. "It's the rules."

"What rules?" Carrie called as her father left the room.

"The rules that say you ain't allowed to see your old man usin' bad language at the sheriff," Pony Simkins advised.

"You children go and get your schoolbooks," Elizabeth said. "That way you'll grow up to be civilized enough to settle your differences in a better fashion."

The children looked as if they thought the fashion currently in use in Shawnee would be more interesting, but under her firm eye, they went.

"Try to make them go to bed at a decent hour," Elizabeth said to Little Deer when the cowboys had followed Tim Ryan outside and she was helping to clear the table. "Oh . . ." She paused. "Little Deer, I didn't think. . . . Do you want to go to this meeting? I didn't mean to leave you to mind the children without asking you."

"You leave children with me," Little Deer said. "I got no use for listening to folks call each other names and fight about cow thieves. That's white people's cows, white people's business. They don't listen to me. Also, that way maybe I don't get shot."

"It can't be that bad," Elizabeth said as they began to wash the dishes. "Surely they were exaggerating."

"I don't know," Little Deer said. "Times getting pretty bad. Mr. Bigelow is a man who can make trouble, and people listen to a man like that." She looked uneasily into her dishwater. "I think he try to make trouble for my people, too. Anyway, I don't go."

Elizabeth was ready at six o'clock. She had no idea what went on at a Shawnee town meeting and wondered if Tim Ryan had been stretching the truth. Occasionally there had been town meetings at home, but no one had ever been shot. She wondered why he had invited her along. As she got into the buggy, she hoped briefly that he might bring up the subject of marriage again, but he did not. They rode in silence all the way into town.

The town hall was crowded and noisy. A red-faced Clyde Sawyer, who as mayor headed the town council, stood at the podium shouting for everyone to be quiet. Independent arguments competed with each other in the din, and no one paid any attention to Clyde.

"We ain't ever gonna get started if you folks don't sit down and save your opinions for the meeting when other folks can hear 'em!" Clyde shouted. He spotted Tim Ryan. "Ryan, you called this. You make 'em come to order."

Ryan stepped up to the podium and yelled, "Shut up!" There was a momentary lull in the uproar, and Ryan picked up Clyde's gavel and banged it on the lectern. "Now you all just sit down, and you'll each get a chance to say your piece."

Most of them sat. Elizabeth found a place next to Lily and Robert Cummings.

Ryan banged the gavel again. "You, too, Bigelow!" he bellowed. "I'm gonna give this gavel back to Clyde, so I won't try to take any advantage." He glared at George Bigelow and stalked to a seat in the front row.

"Is it always like this?" Elizabeth whispered to Lily.

"Mostly," Lily said. "But this time it's serious."

"All right." Clyde Sawyer whapped the gavel on the lectern a few more times for effect. "Now, Tim Ryan's called this meeting because he says that some of our folks hired those guns that tried to burn out Monty Lang's place the other night. We can't have that. If this territory is gonna be a state, we gotta be civilized and do things by the law. And you're gonna enforce it, right, Hank?" He shot a glance at the sheriff, sitting midway down the aisle.

"Of course I am!" Hank Purchase said indignantly. "But I gotta have some proof. I can't go around arresting folks on hearsay."

"Hearsay, hell!" Monty Lang shouted. He was sitting near the front with Pony Simkins on one side of him and Emma on the other. "Of course somebody hired 'em.

They didn't come round to burn me out just 'cause they were looking for something to do."

"You watch your language," Clyde said. "This ain't a saloon. Where's your proof?"

"I know who!" Monty shouted.

"That ain't proof," Clyde said. He had some sympathy for Monty Lang, but he was not ready to tangle with George Bigelow with only Monty's angry assertions to back him up.

"I thought this meeting was about range thieving," Dad Henry said. He glared at Monty Lang. "I ain't got proof either, but someone's been gettin' my cows. If I had proof, I wouldn't be here. I'd be out shooting him!"

"We've all lost cattle," Tim Ryan said. "That's why I called this meeting. But all of you are stirred up against innocent folks. We need to get the proof and go after the right men. What about those three men that got lynched? What if they'd been innocent? You want that on your conscience, Dad?"

"Said I didn't, didn't I?" Dad Henry said.

George Bigelow stood up. "I've lost plenty of cattle," he said. "If you folks had listened to me in the first place, this range wouldn't be so thick with squatters. They're all in league with each other, so finding one cow thief among them is like trying to pick one hornet out of a hive."

"What do you want to do, Bigelow?" Ryan demanded. "Run them all off with a gun and a hangman's noose? They've got the law on their side. Federal law. You go against that, and this territory won't be fit for decent folk to live in."

"Pretty odd talk for an ex-rebel," Bigelow said. "Strikes me you're cutting your coat to suit your cloth, Ryan."

"Bigelow, I'm gonna—"

Clyde Sawyer banged the gavel down again, cutting short a furious muttering from the handful of southerners in the hall. "Keep politics out of this, George, or I'll declare you out of order."

"Bigelow's right," Elias Hamill said. "Seems to me Ryan's on everybody's side but the ranchers. If he had his way, he'd give all our land to Indians and squatters."

"Seems to me people like you want your land and

everybody else's," Tim Ryan said. "I've worked just as hard as any of you, building up my place. I started with nothing, just like most of you. But times change. Frontier's a hard, dangerous place to live, and you don't like it that way. You want to make a safe town, a place that's safe for your wives and kids. Well, you can't do that without people, lots of people, not just a few spread-out ranches. All of those people deserve a share of what we've got."

The town hall erupted into an angry, boiling din as everyone shouted at once.

"Not a share of what I've got!" Hamill snapped.

"Ryan's right!"

"No, he ain't!"

"You can't make a town without givin' folks some stake in it."

"You want Injuns an' coyotes breathin' down your neck for the rest of your life?"

"I don't want squatters breathin' down my neck."

"I'm sick of my stock bein' stole."

"The next man who calls me a thief is gonna step outside an' say it!"

"Well, you sure have defused things, haven't you?" Clyde Sawyer shouted sarcastically to Tim Ryan above the uproar. "What the hell did you call this meeting for, anyway?"

"I thought I could make 'em listen to reason," Ryan muttered.

"Do you think you did any good?" Elizabeth asked Tim Ryan on the drive home. The meeting had resolved nothing. Tempers had flared throughout the evening, and fistfights had barely been avoided.

"Probably not," Ryan said, "but I pointed the finger where I wanted to. If any more hired guns show up, folks'll stop and think about it long enough to take a good look at George Bigelow."

"It sounded to me like most of them agreed with him," Elizabeth said.

"In principle, maybe, but I think they've got enough sense not to act on it with guns and kerosene. I hope so.

Except maybe for that idiot Hamill. Anyway, now Bigelow's men know they've got some opposition, from more folks than just me. Clyde's been working hard to get this territory admitted as a state. He doesn't want a bunch of hotheads botching our chances. Your beau Angus spoke up for our side, too."

"He's not my beau!" Elizabeth snapped.

"Sorry." Ryan drove on silently.

"Why did you invite me to come?" Elizabeth asked after a few minutes.

"I thought it would be educational," Ryan said shortly. "You might as well know what you're in for if you stay."

"I see." Elizabeth thought she saw more than that. She was sure that Tim Ryan wanted George Bigelow to show his true colors, just in case she might have second thoughts. Ryan did not want her himself, but he was determined that George Bigelow not have her either.

Elizabeth awoke the next morning determined to think of Ryan only as an employer. His green, cat-eyed glance—along with certain memories—had troubled her sleep the night before. If she was going to keep on working for him, she could not go dreaming about the house, mentally reliving the night they had spent together. She took a deep breath and decided firmly to be businesslike.

As far as Tim Ryan was concerned, she succeeded in the following days. She was pleasant, friendly, anything but coquettish.

Gradually Ryan began to lose his wariness around her. He had already made love to her, so he did not worry that he might succumb to that temptation. The night they had spent together had defused the situation. He was also relieved that he did not have to marry her. As time passed, they began to be friends.

One day, on a whim, after watching her spoil her clothes by riding Tillie astride, he dragged Caroline's sidesaddle from the loft in the barn, polished it, and gave it to Elizabeth. A divided skirt might have been a more practical gift, but it would not have been proper for him to give her clothes—despite their previous improprieties. He knew she could not afford to buy one herself, so he gave her the saddle and felt good all day after her face lit up in delight. It never occurred to him that, in doing so, he had also said a final good-bye to Caroline.

Elizabeth ran to the barn, got Tillie out of her stall, and put the saddle on her. Ryan helped her mount, and she cantered happily around the ranch yard in figure eights. "Can she jump?" she called to him.

"Yeah," he called back, "but—"

It was too late. Elizabeth turned the mare toward the corral fence, and they sailed over it. She circled the corral at a canter, and sailed back, showing off happily.

"I was going to say, 'Yeah, but can you?' " Ryan said when Elizabeth, breathless and glowing, pulled the mare up beside him.

"Yes," she said, laughing. "I used to hunt at home, when I could borrow a horse."

"It's a wonder to me how women stay on those things."

Elizabeth chuckled. "Men are a mystery. They insist that we are the weaker sex and need taking care of, and then they make us ride dangerous saddles for the sake of propriety."

"Not me," Ryan said indignantly.

"No," Elizabeth said. "Things are different out here, aren't they? For women, too. I've never felt as free as I do here. But I grew up riding a sidesaddle. And I like to jump. You can't do that in a stock saddle. Not very comfortably, anyway. I know," she confessed. "I tried it."

He laughed. "I wish I'd seen that."

"It wasn't very decorous," Elizabeth said. "I made sure no one was around."

"You want to take a ride tomorrow?" Ryan asked suddenly. "Little Deer can watch the kids. I'll take you to meet a friend of mine."

Elizabeth agreed at once.

The next day was Saturday. Elizabeth decided to have Little Deer teach the girls how to make pie crust to keep them busy in her absence. Charlie, lounging disconsolately in the kitchen while Little Deer sifted flour, looked at his mother and Ryan so wistfully that Tim, his finger to his lips, beckoned to him.

"You can come," Ryan whispered. "But slip out of here quietly. If they find out I took you and not them, there'll be a riot."

Charlie flashed him a gleeful smile and ran silently for the barn.

"That was nice of you," Elizabeth told him as they followed Charlie.

"Aw, he oughta have some privileges," Ryan said. "He's the oldest. He's a good boy. Does you credit."

Elizabeth smiled at him, pleased by the compliment. "You're nicer than you let on," she said comfortably.

It was June in Wyoming, clear and beautiful. Under the brilliant blue sky, the prairie grass stretched in rolling, pale-green swells, undulating like a sea toward the soaring mountains. Tim Ryan herded a half-dozen steers—a gift for his friend—through its waves. The air was warm, heavy with the sweet scent of grass. Around each stand of trees, birds fluttered and chirped. Above it all, a hawk soared majestically, riding the air currents. Elizabeth, perched on the sidesaddle, watched the hawk. Charlie lifted his head, his eyes following her gaze.

"What's he looking for?" Charlie asked.

"Lunch," Ryan said. "Field mice, prairie dogs, rabbits when he can get one."

Charlie looked disappointed, envisioning talons fixed on bloody flesh. The hawk was so beautiful. "Why can't he just fly?" he said.

"He's hungry," Elizabeth said. "Besides, we eat rabbits, too."

"I know," Charlie murmured. "But today it just doesn't seem right."

"Everything eats something," Ryan said. "That's life, son."

They rode north toward the mountains and stopped to let the horses drink at an icy little stream that ran down from the foothills. "Nearly there," Ryan said.

"I've never seen an Indian," Charlie said, anticipating the adventure. As they had ridden away from the ranch, Ryan had told them of their destination. They were going to visit Chief Black Wolf. To Charlie, Little Deer, who wore a red Mother Hubbard and gave him cookies, did not count. Real Indians were mysterious and strange. "How will I know how to act?"

"You just be on your company manners," Ryan said. "You'll do fine."

They rounded a stand of trees at the top of a rise. Below them, in a flat valley, the summer encampment of Ryan's friend, Black Wolf, spread before them. A group of tee-pees stood in a close knot around an open area. One large teepee dominated the cluster. A few yards from the teepees, in a sparse stand of trees, several horses grazed in the prairie grass. Ryan herded the cattle down a trail well marked with the bare hooves of Indian ponies, and Charlie and Elizabeth followed.

"You mean anybody can just ride in?" Charlie asked. He had expected something else—menacing braves with spears and scalps on their saddles, or a ring of stern-faced guards with their arrows nocked.

"Oh, they know we're coming," Ryan explained. "Don't worry. They've probably been watching and trailing us for the last ten miles."

"I didn't see anybody."

Ryan chuckled. "You wouldn't." He shooed the steers down the trail and stopped at the bottom of the hill. He raised his hand in salute as a tall man came out from one of the teepees and approached them. Others followed him: men, women, and a few children, all staring at the white woman and her boy and their corn-colored hair.

Elizabeth glanced around nervously. Her tension mounted as she felt their curious eyes on her: the interested eyes of the men, the dark, suspicious eyes of the women. When Ryan told her where they were going, she had been too proud to admit that she was afraid. She recalled the stories she had heard—stories about white women, blonde women, taken captive by Indians, blonde scalps being much prized. Good sense told her that Tim Ryan would not have brought them if it was dangerous. Conquering her fear, she straightened her back and tried to look confident.

"I have brought meat," Ryan said to the tall Indian, who Elizabeth decided must be the chief. "For friendship's sake."

"I thank you," Black Wolf said. "For friendship's sake."

"And I have brought my housekeeper and her son," Ryan said. "They are new to this land and wish to know your ways, so that they too may be friends of the Sioux."

With protocol behind him, Chief Black Wolf turned to his men and spoke to them in the Sioux tongue. The Sioux stared long and silently at Charlie and Elizabeth before they turned and drove the cattle off to one side of the cluster of teepees. "You will come and eat," Black Wolf said. He walked away, following his men, and Ryan motioned Elizabeth to follow.

"Ease up," Ryan murmured. "You look like a petrified rabbit."

"They stare so," Elizabeth whispered.

"They were memorizing your face," he said softly. "That's part of the reason I brought you." As they rode into the settlement, each Indian they passed gave them the same scrutinizing look. White people all looked the same to them. It was important, now that the chief had spoken, that they be certain and remember. Tim Ryan's woman and her pale-haired boy would go unmolested by any man of Black Wolf's tribe.

When Black Wolf stopped in front of the largest teepee, Ryan motioned to Elizabeth and Charlie to dismount. They sat down in the shade of the tent flap while the men butchered one of the steers some distance away, and the women dressed it out. Tim Ryan and his guests would share in the gift they had brought.

Ryan and the chief conversed in low voices, partly in the Sioux language, leaving Elizabeth unable to follow the conversation. She had the feeling that propriety demanded that she not speak unless spoken to. At first she had averted her eyes from the spectacle of the butchered steer, but slowly she looked back, intrigued by the actions of the women and children.

The women, as they dressed the meat, seemed high-spirited, almost gay, calling to each other in melodious, undecipherable words. The children laughed as they circled their mothers, the older children carrying meat or helping lay the fire, the little ones playfully running in rings around the others.

They don't have much meat, Elizabeth realized suddenly. She knew that the Indians hunted buffalo for meat, but the white men hunted the buffalo, too, with bigger, higher-powered guns, driving the buffalo from their natural grazing lands. Where did the buffalo go when the white men took more and more of their range for cattle? She watched the women and little girls pounding out bread to bake and wondered how often bread was all they had to eat. *They are poor*, she thought, *and it's our fault*.

She had thought of herself and the people of Shawnee as pioneers in a new land, but it had been the Indians' land first. Surely there ought to be enough land for everyone in a country this big. As she watched the children laughing hungrily at the meat sizzling on a spit over the fire, she knew that if it were left to the big ranchers like George Bigelow and Elias Hamill, maybe even to homesteaders like Monty Lang and his Emma, or Inga and her sister, all eager to better themselves, there would not be enough land. Not as more and more white people came with every stagecoach and wagon train. *No wonder they want to fight us*. She looked at Ryan, talking to Black Wolf. He knew it; he was just trying to stave it off as long as he could. She tried to catch the gist of their talk.

"Maybe you're right," Ryan was saying. "If you're not right now, then I think you will be soon. But just now my kind are quarreling among themselves. Use the time, if you can, for a respite."

"And when the respite is gone?" Black Wolf said. "What then?"

Ryan sighed. "I don't know. I've done the best I can. But preaching fairness to men who are land hungry is a losing battle."

"It is not men I fear," Black Wolf said with a dark smile. "It is women." He looked at Elizabeth, a knowing, thoughtful look. "When the white man brings white women, then he builds towns. And where there are towns, other white men spread out from them in widening circles to find more land. It has been thus so far. It will not change."

"And then?" Ryan said.

"And then, my friend, you know as well as I. Can any man take sides against his own people in a war? Not I. And not, I think, you."

"No," Ryan said somberly.

"But for now, while there is no war," Black Wolf said, "we may enjoy the day. It is a feast day because our friend has come, and our friend's friends. Soon we will eat."

A little girl the twins' age went by, proudly carrying a plate of meat. She smiled shyly at Charlie, and Charlie smiled back. She was pretty, with red thongs braided into her long black hair.

"She smiled at me," Charlie whispered. "Look, Mama!"

I wish we could just leave it to the children, Elizabeth thought. Could the children—white and Indian—grow together in peace? Or would the children grow to discover their differences and not be friends?

"What is it like, this land that you have come from, Tim Ryan's woman?" Black Wolf said.

Elizabeth started to say that she was not Tim Ryan's woman, but a look from him told her to let it go by. "It is beautiful," she said to Black Wolf. "Not beautiful in the same way as your land, but still very beautiful. There are many trees and rivers, many rivers, and many little streams. The trees have flowers in the spring."

"Are the flowers good to eat?"

"No," Elizabeth said. "Only pretty."

"Ah. That too has its purpose."

"And there are towns, with white houses, or houses made of brick, with little green lawns and white fences around them." Elizabeth gazed into the distance, wistfully remembering. "We plant flowers in gardens, so that every spring and summer there are flowers everywhere. All along the brick sidewalks there are wooden boxes with flowers in them. All the houses have lace curtains." It was an exaggerated picture of harmony and domesticity, but very real in her mind.

"You see," Black Wolf said gently to Tim Ryan. "You see, my friend, why it is that I fear the women."

"I've got lace curtains in my own damn house," Ryan said, knowing nevertheless that his friend was right.

That night Tim Ryan woke up, shaking. It was dark, and a sliver of moonlight gleamed in the window, spilling onto the coverlet on the bed, just the way it had been in his dream. His heart was pounding, and his hair was damp with sweat. He could keep Elizabeth Bradley in her proper place as his housekeeper during the daytime, but he could not keep her clothes on her in his dreams. This dream was uncannily like the one he had on the night she arrived at the Broken R. Surprisingly, Caroline had not been in this one, and a lot more had happened between him and Elizabeth—in fact, exactly what had happened between them a couple of weeks ago.

Ryan wiped his face with his hands and lay back on his pillow. He wondered if Elizabeth would know he had been dreaming about her simply by looking at him. He hoped not.

Caroline had not been in it. He mulled that thought over. It was the first dream he had had since she left that she had not been in. Maybe he was cured, not just of loving her, but of hating her, too. Maybe it was time he considered marrying again.

But he was damned, he thought sleepily, if he would waste his time courting a woman who had turned him down.

Meg Callahan drove her stylish landau along the dirt road toward the Broken R the next day. The setter pup, which appeared to favor its unknown father considerably more than its mother, was beside her in a box on the floor. Its eyes were open now, and it had grown fat and sassy, altogether a healthy specimen of whatever it was.

She flicked the reins nervously, hurrying the horse along. Meg, who was never less than elegantly turned out, was particularly stylish today in a jonquil yellow driving costume of ribbed silk, with a black lace bow at her throat and a jaunty little hat with a wing of black feathers. She was aware that respectable women would think she was too overdressed to deliver a dog, but she did not care. She was more concerned with what Tim Ryan was going to think about her delivering the dog at all. She had heard all the bets and rumors: how Tim Ryan had given his housekeeper his wife's sidesaddle; how he took her riding; how he had a gleam in his eye. Meg had to see it for herself.

When she drove up, Ryan was in the yard. He looked up at her, startled, and then waved. Meg's heart turned over, but she climbed out of the landau as if nothing bothered her. "I brought your pup back," she said quickly before Ryan could ask her why she had come.

Ryan pushed his hat back on his head, looking down into the box. "That's no dog; it's a hyena," he said.

"I didn't say he was a beauty," Meg said. "But he's healthy. He'll do fine with the rest of 'em now."

"Here, you girls, come here," he yelled, and Carrie and Susannah jumped off the swing and ran over. "I got something for you. You take him in to Frieda and stay with her until you're sure she'll take to him."

"Yes, sir!" Carrie scooped the box up in both arms. "Come on, let's go show him to Miss 'Lizabeth first!" They ran off toward the house.

Meg's mouth twisted. She looked toward the house and saw Elizabeth Bradley in the open doorway, with the girls running toward her.

Ryan held his hand out. "I want to thank you—"

On an impulse, Meg quickly took his hand in hers and pulled it around her waist. She leaned toward him and kissed him on the lips, long and passionately.

Ryan did not move. He did not kiss her, either. He just stood there, confused. When she let go of him, he smiled at her vaguely. Behind him, the door of the house had closed. Elizabeth Bradley was gone.

"I gotta go," Meg muttered.

"Thank you for taking care of the pup," he said, as if he were trying to offer her something that they both knew was not what she had wanted.

Meg climbed into the landau and shook out the reins. She could feel tears running down her cheeks. She whipped the horse into a canter. That had been a rotten, wicked thing to do, kissing him like that so Mrs. Bradley would see. Tim Ryan did not want her, so she had deliberately tried to spoil what she thought he did want. She was ashamed of herself. Meg sobbed harder.

Chapter Ten

Elizabeth spent the next three weeks trying to forget that she had seen Tim Ryan kissing Meg Callahan in the Broken R yard. By the time the Fourth of July came along, she had nearly managed it, or so she told herself.

Shawnee had always celebrated the Fourth of July with great enthusiasm, and folks had been working hard to make this year's celebration one of the town's best. Everyone at the Broken R had gotten up early that morning to do their chores quickly and get themselves ready for the festivities. Driving the buggy into Shawnee with the children, Elizabeth was surrounded by a cloud of dust and a lively group of whooping, excited cowboys who were ready to celebrate.

In Shawnee, all the false fronts of the buildings were hung with swags of red, white, and blue bunting. A white banner with red letters that read Shawnee Celebrates Independence Day had been stretched across the street from Fishburn's store to the Sawyer House Hotel. Atop the opera house cupola, the Stars and Stripes were flying above the flag of Wyoming Territory, and a band was playing in the street outside it. The band was composed of two fiddlers, a trombone, and Angus Ogilvie wailing on the bagpipes. All along the sidewalk, booths selling lemonade, ice cream, and homemade pies had been set up. On the lawn of St. Peter's, a whole steer was roasting on a spit for the evening barbecue. Behind the firepit, long tables covered with bed sheets had been arranged. Tickets to the dinner would benefit the Parish House Construction Fund.

Tim Ryan and the rest of the cowboys rode their horses into the school yard, and Elizabeth turned the buggy in after them. They found places to hitch the horses among the crowd of horses, buggies, and wagons already there.

"Oh, boy!" Charlie, his eyes shining, jumped out of the buggy, and the twins scrambled down behind him. Each of the children had a dollar to spend.

"Now just wait a minute!" Elizabeth quickly grabbed at the three of them. "You all stay out of the saloon and any other place you know I don't want you to go, and don't go past the far end of the sidewalk." Farther down the street, beyond the stage depot, Elizabeth could hear sounds of more raucous celebration.

"Yes, ma'am." They danced excitedly as she told them the rest of the rules.

"Be back here when they ring the bell for dinner." She looked at them doubtfully. "And try to stay clean."

"Yes, ma'am!" They raced down the street toward the band and the ice cream booth.

"Don't they look nice!" Elizabeth said to Ryan, as she watched them go. The twins had on their best pinafores; their hair had been brushed into dark ringlets.

"That they do," he agreed. "You may turn them into ladies yet, but if you think they're gonna stay clean, you're living in a fool's paradise. There'll be sack races later on."

"I'm not a complete idiot," Elizabeth said. "Their clothes for the dance tonight are in here." She patted a carpetbag tucked in the back of the buggy.

"Is that what you've been sewing on all week?"

"It is. And wait until you see what I've made for them!" With Ryan's approval she had spent his money liberally in Fishburn's and bought taffeta for the girls' first real party dresses: blue for Carrie and yellow for Susannah. They looked adorable dressed alike, but Elizabeth felt it was time they realized that they were two different people.

"Well, they'll be in demand," Ryan said. "We never have enough women to go around." He strolled off down the street.

Elizabeth, left to her own devices, saw Lily Cummings waving at her from the baked goods table. Each booth sponsored a charity, and Lily's was for the benefit of the Women's Library Committee. There was no library in Shawnee, but Lily intended to change that.

The band was playing a free version of "Old Dan Tucker," and Lily had to shout to make herself heard above the noise. "I haven't seen you in so long." She patted Elizabeth's hand. "Quite a celebration, isn't it?"

As far as Elizabeth could tell, everyone in Shawnee was there: cowboys, businessmen, wives, the saloon girls, and even Meg Callahan's girls, strolling under silk parasols. All the outlying ranchers and homesteaders had come for the celebration. Children were everywhere, underfoot, dribbling ice cream on their elders, and lining up for the egg-and-spoon race.

Elizabeth saw Beth Armstrong, the schoolteacher, strolling on the arm of her intended in a red and white dress that was much more dashing than anything she would have dared to wear while she was still employed by the school board. The new teacher was due to arrive in the fall, and Lily predicted that she would not last more than a year, either. Women never did out here, unless they were totally ugly, and then it took two years.

The band had switched to "Oh, Susannah," and two cowboys were dancing exuberantly with each other to the music. Elizabeth saw a trio of Indians standing outside the hotel, watching the crowd with solemn, unreadable expressions.

"What do you suppose they think of it all?" Elizabeth asked Lily.

Lily giggled. "Heaven only knows. They'll probably be better behaved than our people, I'm sorry to say."

"Will there be trouble?" Elizabeth asked.

"Probably a few fistfights," Lily said. "There always are." She looked pensive. "I'd feel better, though, if everyone weren't so jumpy. The most amazing rumors have been floating around ever since the town meeting. They're all seeing Indians and rustlers over their shoulders. Some people don't have any sense."

*   *   *

Tim Ryan, making his rounds of the celebration, picked up the fearful tension that Lily had described to Elizabeth. Sheriff Hank Purchase was wearing two guns. When Ryan raised his eyebrows, Hank muttered darkly of Indian attack.

"Well, those'll do just fine to fend 'em off," Ryan said, nodding at Hank's guns. "Providing you don't hit somebody's wife by mistake."

"I got a town to protect," Hank said righteously. "Wouldn't be surprised if those squatter cow thieves weren't out an' about, too, while law-abiding folk are celebratin' their heritage."

"The homesteaders are all in town, celebrating along with everybody else," Ryan said disgustedly.

He dropped in on a poker game in the Sawyer House saloon and heard more of the same from Elias Hamill. He then had a drink with Seth Hawks, a middle-aged homesteader, who was packing a gun, too.

"Not you, too, Seth."

"I heard there were more hired guns comin'," Seth said. He spat into the brass cuspidor by the bar. "Nobody's runnin' me offa my land, white or Injun."

"You seen any Indians?"

"I heard talk," Seth said. "It's all over town."

"And the hired guns? Where'd you hear about them?"

"Hell, I don't know. Everybody's talkin'. I heard the cattlemen are bringin' 'em in. What you got to say about that, Ryan?"

"I'll have a lot to say when I find out who started all this idiot talk."

"You ain't gonna find out," Clyde Sawyer said. He was working behind the bar today, keeping an eye on things. "Everybody in town's got a theory, and none of 'em make any more sense than the rest. You and your damn town meeting. You got 'em stirred up good."

"There's more to it than that," Ryan answered. "Things calmed down a little after that meeting, and now they're all riled up again. Somebody's feeding these rumors, Clyde."

"Hell, they got a life of their own, now," Clyde said.

"Everybody's lookin' over their shoulder. They'll be seeing ghosts next."

"I'm gonna get to the bottom of this," Ryan said. "The body I've got in mind isn't any ghost, but I'm gonna qualify him for that honor if I get my hands on him."

"I know what you're thinking," Clyde said, "but you can't prove it."

"Then it's time I bring in someone who can," Ryan replied.

When he ran into Monty Lang outside the Sawyer House and heard what Monty had to say, Ryan knew he had to act. Monty held a frightened Emma on his arm. He told Ryan that someone had just left a bloody stillborn calf in their wagon. It had a noose around its neck.

"That does it." Ryan stalked across the street to the telegraph office at the stage depot, giving Hank Purchase a baleful glare as he passed him.

"That's gonna cost you a pretty penny," the telegraph operator said to Ryan when he had written out his message.

"Just send it," Tim growled. "I didn't spend six months last year agitating to get that wire strung out here to worry about the price of the service. I must've bought a quart of whiskey for every politician in Cheyenne. This'll be cheap by comparison."

The telegraph operator shrugged. He took Ryan's money and started clicking out the message:

TO FEDERAL MARSHAL CHEYENNE STOP URGENTLY REQUEST YOU COME TO SHAWNEE AS SOON AS POSSIBLE STOP TROUBLE COMING BETWEEN CATTLEMEN AND HOMESTEADERS STOP THERE HAVE BEEN HIRED GUNS AND ONE BARN BURNING STOP POSSIBLY TROUBLE WITH INDIANS TOO STOP INDIANS HAVE NOT PROVOKED IT STOP WE WANT END PUT TO IT BY IMPARTIAL LAW ENFORCEMENT WHICH WE HAVE NOT GOT STOP URGENTLY REQUEST YOU COME REPEAT URGENTLY STOP TIMOTHY RYAN BROKEN R RANCH SHAWNEE STOP

At the evening barbecue, Ryan watched as the citizens of Shawnee continued to glare at each other suspiciously over their tin plates of barbecued beef. However, the presence of the Reverend Mr. William Leslie and the prospect of the coming dance in the opera house put a damper on open belligerence. Nobody wanted to miss the dance.

When the children had finished their dinner, Elizabeth sent Charlie to the Sawyer House, where the men were changing their clothes, with Ryan and John Potter. She took the girls to the schoolhouse, which had been reserved for the women.

The schoolhouse was jammed with laughing, chatting women, who were bustling about, buttoning each other's dresses and helping to arrange each other's hair. They were on considerably better terms with each other than were the men. *If we had more women, there wouldn't be all this nonsense*, Elizabeth thought. Women could vote in Wyoming, but they were heavily outnumbered by the men. Perhaps most of them voted the way their husbands told them to. George Bigelow, for instance, would believe that he had married the vote along with the woman.

Every woman who could possibly afford it had a new dress, Elizabeth observed. Emma Lang's face looked strained, but she had a pretty new dress of red calico. Elizabeth, having scrubbed the girls thoroughly at the schoolhouse pump, helped Carrie and Susannah into their new dresses and told them to stand still and not to sit down. As Elizabeth watched, they went to admire themselves in a full-length mirror that someone had thoughtfully provided. They were thrilled with the new dresses. *Perhaps a sign of growing femininity*, Elizabeth thought hopefully.

She shook out her own new gown, made from the old rose silk ballgown that she had brought with her to Wyoming. She had picked out the seams of the skirt and used its twenty yards of silk to cut a new dress. She had trimmed the square neck, the cap sleeves, the draped apron, and the short train with lace salvaged from the old gown and with petals she had cut from an expensive, precious yard of pale green taffeta. The pink roses that had ornamented the neckline of the old gown were now pinned on one shoulder with her mother's pearl brooch. It was a

dashing toilette, possibly too dashing, she thought with
mild worry, for a housekeeper in Shawnee. But Lily Cummings had pronounced it perfect when Elizabeth had
proudly shown it to her before dinner.

The men were waiting in the opera house when the
women arrived. Some of the ranchers and businessmen
had donned evening clothes, many of them years out of
style, and the cowboys had put on clean shirts and slicked
their hair down. Dad Henry had his new false teeth in,
and Angus Ogilvie had trimmed his beard and was wearing a kilt. (The look in his eye dared any cowboy to make
so much as one remark.) To a man, they were ready for
female company.

It did not matter what age the women were. From
Carrie and Susannah to old Mrs. Sawyer, Clyde's mother,
who practically had to be carried around the dance floor,
they were immediately claimed by eager partners as the
fiddlers struck up a Virginia reel. Even so there were not
enough women to go around. To make up enough couples,
some of the cowboys were taking turns being "heifer
branded" with frilly aprons and dancing with each other.
As Elizabeth danced down the reel with Angus Ogilvie,
she saw Bill Ennis and Pony Simkins galumphing through
the figure just ahead of them. Carrie was dancing with
John Potter, and Susannah with their father. The twins'
eyes were shining excitedly.

Elizabeth let herself be swept along by the music. It
had been so long since she had danced. When the fiddlers
ended the reel and struck up a waltz, she found Angus
Ogilvie's place taken by Tim Ryan, slim and elegant
and somehow unlike himself in a long-tailed coat. Ex-
tending his hand gravely, he bowed, and she danced into
his arms.

"You're a very accomplished dancer," he commented
after a minute.

"I had years of lessons," Elizabeth said. "Every lady
should be an accomplished dancer. That was what my
mother said. You remember what it was like before the
war—I wasn't supposed to have much else to worry about."
She smiled at him mistily. "I will not become maudlin. It's

too lovely tonight." She hummed softly to the music as they spun and circled about the lamplit room.

"I told you there wouldn't be enough women to go around," Ryan said as two cowboys swooped by, dancing with each other. The one in the apron was holding it by one corner with his little finger sticking out and was doing what Elizabeth suspected was a devilish imitation of Agnes Sawyer's dancing style. "If everyone wasn't too fine haired to let the saloon girls and Meg's gals come, there'd be plenty of partners."

Elizabeth stiffened, all her pleasure in the dance draining from her. She was silent for the rest of the dance. When it ended, Robert Cummings claimed her for the next reel. She turned to him with relief. *I will have a good time*, she thought defiantly, dancing away down the line with Robert. *I don't care who he wishes were here. He can just go to that . . . that cathouse, and dance with her if he wants to!* She gave Robert her best smile and picked up her skirts, sashaying in and out of the pattern with determined gaiety.

Ryan asked her for one more dance, but he found it was like dancing with a wooden doll, and he gave up dancing with her after that. What in hell had come over her, he wondered, frowning. He danced with Carrie and then retired moodily to the punch bowl for a drink. By now someone was certain to have spiked it with whiskey.

"Little housekeeper didn't look none too friendly," Cal Hodges observed. He was lounging by the punch bowl, watching the dancers.

Ryan glared at him. "She's not your business!" he snapped.

When the fiddlers struck up "Skip to My Lou," Elizabeth saw George Bigelow approaching her with the confident expression of a man who would not be refused. She hastily gave her hand to Bill Ennis, who was handy. Dancing with Bigelow would make Tim Ryan angry, but she would not do it, not after what Bigelow had done to Monty and Emma Lang.

> Lost my partner, what'll I do?
> Skip to my Lou, my darlin'!

The "extra" man circled inside the ring, pulled Lily Cummings out of it, and danced down the inside of the circle with her. Lily's partner, old Dad Henry, cavorted off inside the ring to "steal" a new lady.

> I'll get another one, prettier than you,
> Skip to my Lou, my darlin'!

Each new couple circled the ring until they came to an open place in the moving line of dancers, while the others moved behind them, each man who lost his partner picking a new one from the line.

> Pretty as a redbird, prettier too!
> Can't get a redbird, a bluebird'll do!
> Gone again! What'll I do?
> Skip to my Lou, my darlin'!

It was a lively dance, and the cowboys put their backs into it, competing with each other for the open spaces and the prettiest girls. Elizabeth found herself plucked out of the line by George Bigelow and whisked off on his arm.

"I trust you will grant me the privilege of a somewhat tamer dance later on," he said.

They swung around and took their places in the line again.

"I'm terribly sorry, but they are all taken," Elizabeth said, knowing he did not believe her. How could they be taken, when nobody had a dance card?

"A pity." Bigelow cast an appraising eye at Tim Ryan on the sidelines. "May one ask by whom?"

"No," Elizabeth said shortly, and with relief gave her arm to Angus Ogilvie.

Bigelow did not ask her again, but Elizabeth had no shortage of partners. After a few more turns, she found herself to her dismay with Cal Hodges.

"Well, now," Cal said, "I reckon you can step out pretty."

He smelled of whiskey, and she was not sure he was listening to her.

"I'm feeling rather tired," Elizabeth said. Cal paid no attention. He pulled her to him roughly and began to dance.

"I heard you give old Bigelow the brush-off," Cal said as the fiddler called, *Swing your partners!* "Now that was smart. I can give you a better time than he can."

He was holding her too tightly, tighter than propriety allowed, and Elizabeth felt flushed and conspicuous. The evening, which had begun so nicely, had turned sour and unpleasant. Cal's voice made her skin crawl, and with outrage she felt his hand slide down over her buttocks.

"Bigelow don't know how to go about pleasin' a woman," Cal slurred. "But I do."

That was too much. Elizabeth pulled away from him and smacked the palm of her hand across Cal's face, hard, putting all her anger for Tim Ryan and George Bigelow into it as well.

The sound rung in the silence of a momentary pause in the music. Every head in the room whirled around to look, and the fiddlers stopped playing. Cal, in an almost visible cloud of whiskey, grabbed her by the shoulder, ripping the lace and the green silk leaves away from her sleeve.

"What the hell's holding you back?" he demanded loudly. "Ain't I good enough? Or ain't I got enough money to suit you?" He looked for some further insult to hurl and made a lucky guess. "It ain't your reputation, is it? Not after the way you been carryin' on with the boss."

Elizabeth, the color draining from her cheeks, shoved him away from her.

Cal staggered back a step or two and then felt himself spun around by one shoulder. When Tim Ryan's fist connected with his jaw, Cal was hurled backward and crashed onto the dance floor. Before he could pick himself up, Ryan lifted him by his pants and collar and flung him through the open door.

"You're fired!" Ryan shouted after him.

Everyone in the silent room was looking at Elizabeth Bradley, some with sympathy and some with speculation.

She stared horror stricken at Tim Ryan, turned and pushed through the ring of dancers, and fled out a side door into the cool, concealing darkness of the night.

Behind her she heard the music start up again, raggedly at first and then with self-conscious jollity. *Skip to my Lou!* There was a bale of hay in the yard beside the opera house—the livery stable was next door—and she sat down on it, her cheeks burning and her thoughts swirling.

How could Ryan have done that to her? Cal Hodges was bad enough, but Ryan's reaction to Cal would convince everybody in Shawnee that Cal had been right. Obviously, Elizabeth thought miserably, Ryan did not care about that or about her. He could not care that her reputation in Shawnee was now irrevocably ruined—as ruined as Ryan's hypothetical maiden with the broken buggy axle.

Clearly, Ryan was not going to ask her to marry him now. Every respectable person in Shawnee would say that Elizabeth Bradley was good enough for Tim Ryan to sleep with, but not good enough for him to marry. She would be relegated to the social status of the saloon girls, and Charlie's life would be ruined. Even Carrie and Susannah would suffer over the gossip about their governess and their father. Elizabeth blinked back tears. She would have to go home. Home to Virginia. There was nothing else to do.

A shadow fell across the straw at her feet, and she looked up to see George Bigelow, his solid frame black against the light from the opera house windows.

"My dear." George sat down beside her on the bale of hay. "Tim Ryan has never been noted for his tact," he commented.

"That is my problem, Mr. Bigelow," Elizabeth said stiffly.

"My dear, allow me to make it mine," he said. "You will admit that you are in need of some assistance. That you should be subjected to such a scene is unconscionable. I had meant to continue my courting for a few more months, as soon as the recent unpleasantness over that lying cow thief Lang had died down, and you were more inclined to see things from my viewpoint. But under the circumstances, uh, perhaps I should get on with it. I've come out here to propose, my dear. A quick marriage to me should stop even the hastiest tongue."

Elizabeth looked up at him. From the open window, the music came softly.

> Lost my partner, what'll I do?
> I'll get another one, prettier than you!

If she married George Bigelow, no one would talk about her, Elizabeth thought. If she married George Bigelow, she would have money, and Charlie would have good schools and college. Tears rolled down her cheeks.

"No," she said faintly.

"You'd better think carefully about this," he said conversationally. "You are going to be talked about, you know. Fairly spitefully, I might add, thanks to Ryan and his drunken cowhand."

He paused and then continued. "You will notice that I am not even going to ask whether that story is true. I know you well enough to know what sort of behavior I could expect of you as my wife. I require a woman of breeding and beauty and social poise, and you fulfill those requirements admirably.

"I am going to go places, Elizabeth, when I have the right woman beside me. That woman could be you. If I were you, I would think twice before I passed up a life of ease and promise."

"I am thinking," Elizabeth said. There was no point in telling him how she felt about his conduct toward the homesteaders; no point in calling him a brigand, which he was.

"I don't love you, George," she said flatly as she rose. "I married a man I didn't love the first time, and it made my life miserable. I won't do it again. If I marry again, it will be for love, or I will stay single."

George Bigelow stared at her in the dim light, his expression growing more exasperated. "I should have known it," he said. "Cal Hodges has about enough brains to operate his mouth, but occasionally it takes a fool to point out what's under everyone's nose." He stood up. "But I'll give you a warning, my dear. If you're in love with Tim Ryan, you'll be a very old lady before he ever marries you!" He turned on his heel and stalked off, jamming his hat down over his eyes.

After a moment, she heard the buggy wheels rattling in the street. Elizabeth again sat wearily on the bale of hay. So much for ease and promise. While she felt a small flicker of regret for Bigelow's money, she felt also unutterable relief that she had not succumbed to its temptation. George Bigelow was ruthless, not just to the homesteaders or the Indians, but to anyone who stood in his way. She had had a small personal taste of that ruthlessness tonight. He did not love her; he just wanted her. Once she had married him, life with George Bigelow would have been worse than anything she had lived through with Charles.

She stood up. He had been right about Ryan, though, and right about the gossip. Since she was not going to take George Bigelow for a shield, she would have to leave Shawnee. But before she left, she would tell Lily that she had turned Bigelow down, she thought with a tearful grin. Lily would be sure to spread it around, and a rumor like that might tone down the talk. A desperate, ruined woman would not throw George Bigelow away. It would also make Bigelow angry, and he richly deserved that.

Elizabeth straightened her hair. She would have to leave, but in the meantime she would hold her head up, for the children's sake. It was the only weapon she had. She marched back into the hall.

Meg Callahan sat on the red velvet settee in her parlor, moodily sipping a whiskey and water. Her slim feet were propped on the end of the settee, and the flounces of her elegant dress cascaded over her ankles. The expression on her face was anything but seductive. She brooded as she listened to Elias Hamill, a rancher who never stayed long at any respectable party when there was livelier amusement to be had, roar with laughter over by the piano, giving the piano player and two of Meg's girls a firsthand account of the happening at the opera house.

"By God, you shoulda seen it! I got no use for Tim Ryan, but by God you shoulda seen him pick up that cowhand and throw him right out the damn door! And Agnes Sawyer and her old mother-in-law, standing there with their prissy mouths wide open wondering how their party had got so outta hand. An' then Mrs. Bradley flew out the other door, and all the other little biddies were runnin' around like a buncha wet hens, not knowin' whether to be mad at the cowhand for takin' liberties, or at Mrs. Bradley for causin' a brawl, or at Tim Ryan for brawlin' in the opera house. After that, I figured nothing else as interesting was gonna happen, so I come on over here. Which one o' you lil darlin's is gonna entertain me?"

The girls giggled appreciatively. Since they had not been invited to the dance in the opera house, the discomfort of the respectable ladies of the town amused them.

Meg stroked McKinley, the raccoon, who was asleep in her lap. He was a small, furry comfort in the midst of her melancholy. If Tim Ryan had tossed Cal Hodges bodily out the door, Meg had no illusions about why. Ryan had never had a hasty temper. If he had developed one tonight it was not just because Cal had insulted his housekeeper. Tim Ryan was in love; Meg was sure of it.

"Hell, that ain't all of it," said a cowboy who had just come in and heard the end of Hamill's story. "I went out right afterward, an—"

"Ryan throw you out, too?" someone asked, chuckling.

"I was lookin' for the privy, you fool, only I'm too delicate minded to say so here in front of ladies. Anyway, I went out. Old Cal Hodges wasn't anywheres in sight. But there was George Bigelow, sittin' on a bale of hay, proposin' to Mrs. Bradley."

"The hell you say!" Meg's girls and their customers gathered around him, interested in this latest development. The piano player stopped playing and swiveled around on his stool.

"Big as life, offerin' her his heart an' hand."

"George Bigelow ain't got no heart!" someone guffawed.

"Well, he's got a lot of money in the hand, so I reckon it didn't make no difference," another said.

"Now, that's where you're wrong," the cowboy replied. "I just kinda scrunched up in the porch and listened, and do you know what she said? Said she didn't love him."

"Hell, who does?" Hamill chortled.

"I think that's romantic," Sadie said with a sigh.

"I think she's one brick shy of a load, that's what I think," Lucy said. "I'd marry an Indian if he had as much money as George Bigelow."

"I wonder what Bigelow wants with her," Hamill said, "if she's ruined an' all."

"Maybe he thinks she ain't ruined," the cowboy said.

"Livin' out there with Tim Ryan?" Hamill whooped. "Ryan used to be the randiest devil in the territory. He toned down some when he got married, but a leopard don't change his spots. I reckon old Cal knew what he was talking about. What do you think, Meg? Ryan used to be a pal of yours."

"I think it's none of your damn business!" Meg snapped.

"A thousand pardons." Hamill turned his back on her ostentatiously, hands in his pockets, whistling. He was in a mood to devil her tonight. He had always been a little jealous of Tim Ryan, particularly of Meg's fondness for him.

Meg had known Elias Hamill almost as long as she had known Ryan, and at one time Elias Hamill had courted her, before she had gone into the parlor house business.

At least Elias doesn't moon around like a lovesick schoolgirl, Meg thought miserably. *Which is what I've been doing. Tim's in love with that woman, and she's in love with him, or she wouldn't have turned down George Bigelow. I should be cheering that Tim's found a decent woman, not a witch like Caroline, instead of trying to break them up.* Meg bit her lip so she would not cry in front of her customers.

Thoughtfully, she scratched McKinley's ears. "I'm ashamed of myself, McKinley, that's what I am," she said. She looked around the room. The piano player had begun a tune, and her girls and the men were dancing to it.

Some of the men, Elias Hamill for instance, were as handsome as Tim Ryan and nearly as successful. Meg put McKinley down on the floor. It was time to get rid of her fantasies, she thought, and then get on with living.

She went over to Elias Hamill. "You still remember how to dance?" she asked him.

Chapter Eleven

Cal Hodges was in a rage. That fist to his jaw and the humiliation of Ryan throwing him out of the dance had sobered him. No one treated Cal Hodges that way. He knew he had to pay Ryan back, and he knew just the right man to help him do a good job of it.

He whipped his horse to a headlong gallop, not caring if it stumbled and broke both their necks. His horse's hooves thundered across the ground. When he got to George Bigelow's Double X spread, he tied the horse to the front rail and pounded on the door.

"The boss ain't home," Bigelow's cook said, when he had dragged the door open.

"I know he ain't," Cal said. He pushed past the cook. "I'm gonna wait for him."

"You could be waitin' a while," the cook said. "Sometimes he sleeps in town."

"I'll wait," Cal said stubbornly.

George Bigelow drove home, his mouth set in an exasperated line. When he found Cal Hodges in his office, his boots on the desk, the exasperated look changed to one of fury.

"I oughta punch your lights out," Bigelow snarled.

"I'm here to do you a favor, Bigelow," Cal said. "You oughta be grateful."

"Get your boots off my desk," Bigelow ordered.

"Sure," Cal said. He swung his feet down. "I'm lookin' for a job."

"And get out of my chair." Bigelow sat down in the chair that Cal vacated. He raised his eyebrows. "That's a favor? You aren't any prize, Hodges."

"That's all you know," Cal said. "I'll do just about any work you've got in mind, long as it does that bastard Ryan one in the eye. Might turn out to be a big favor."

Bigelow cooled down and looked thoughtful. "It might at that," he agreed after a moment. He might just kill two birds with one stone, while he was at it. George Bigelow was not a man to let what he wanted—and that included a woman—escape him. Elizabeth Bradley would thank him for his persistence once she had married him.

"I want to find out what Mrs. Bradley's up to for the next couple of days," Bigelow said. "Find out when she's planning to go into town next, without Ryan." He gave Cal a warning look. "But stay away from her. Ask around."

"I don't want nothing to do with her," Cal muttered. "Prideful bitch. But I don't need to ask around, I already know. I heard her tell Mrs. Cummings she was coming for a visit tomorrow. Why you want to know?"

Bigelow grinned. *All the better,* he thought. "Because you're gonna see she doesn't get there. She's coming here instead."

Cal tossed his head back. "I reckon I'd enjoy that. But I ain't about to get strung up for kidnapping."

"You aren't going to," Bigelow said. "Indians are going to kidnap poor Mrs. Bradley. Don't you think you'd make a dandy Indian, Cal?"

An hour later, George Bigelow walked Cal over to the Double X bunkhouse. Cal was grinning in the moonlight.

"Just one thing, Hodges," Bigelow said. "One word in your ear. I am planning to marry Mrs. Bradley. You can shake her up enough to make her grateful for my appearance, but you'd better not touch her. You touch her, Hodges, and you won't live to get paid."

*   *   *

After breakfast the next morning, Elizabeth swung the buggy out of the yard and headed for town. The twins were hunting for eggs in the hayloft because Little Deer had promised that she would make them a custard if they did. At the last minute Elizabeth had asked Charlie to come with her. After the previous night's disaster, she felt too forlorn and lonely to make the long drive into Shawnee with only her own unhappy thoughts for company.

When she had made her plans with Lily yesterday afternoon, she had been looking forward to a nice adult conversation. Now, instead of gossiping, she was going to ask Lily to lend her train fare home. She had not saved enough from her salary, and she could not wait until she had. Somehow, she would pay Lily back.

Elizabeth sighed. She could not leave without telling Ryan, of course, but she knew it would be better if she were packed, with tickets in hand, before she confronted him.

The drive home from Shawnee the night before had been ghastly. Ryan had been taciturn and, she thought, maybe a little drunk, riding on Beau beside the buggy. Elizabeth had huddled in the buggy and let Tillie do the navigating.

Charlie broke into her thoughts and asked quietly now as they drove, "Mama, are you mad at Cal Hodges?"

"Yes."

"Are you mad at Mr. Ryan too?" Charlie's small face was puzzled.

"Yes. No. Mr. Ryan and I haven't been getting along very well lately."

"Oh," Charlie said sadly. "I like Mr. Ryan," he added. "Maybe you'll make up?"

"I don't know, dear," Elizabeth said.

Elizabeth knew how much Charlie loved Wyoming. *How can I make him leave here?* she thought desolately. *How can I take him back to Virginia? I've ruined all his chances because I was fool enough to fall into bed with Tim Ryan.*

Tillie's hooves clip-clopped on the ground. The road was poor here, just a packed-down trail across the open prairie, with grass stunted by the infrequent traffic. Except for a hawk sailing above them, Charlie and the horse were the only living things that Elizabeth could see. The stand of trees growing by the little stream that was the cause of contention between Monty Lang and George Bigelow made the only break in the flatness of the prairie until her eyes reached the mountains.

As they neared the trees, Tillie threw up her head and snorted. Warily, Elizabeth reached for the rifle that Ryan always insisted she take with her. A dozen riders exploded from the trees. She snatched the gun up frantically and then lowered it as the leading rider pointed a rifle at her and shouted, "Drop it!"

Elizabeth's heart turned over. Indians! Were they Black Wolf's men? If they were, would they recognize her? Would they care? Their dark faces were splashed with war paint, and she could not tell if she had ever seen any of them before.

"What do you want?" she cried, terrified. The leader bent down from his pinto and sliced Tillie's reins with a knife. He circled around behind the buggy. Another Indian caught up the cut reins and brought the horse and buggy to a halt. No one answered her.

"Get him out!" one of them shouted from behind her. A third Indian reached into the buggy, dragged a kicking Charlie out, and dumped him on the ground.

"Charlie!" she yelled.

One of the men smacked Tillie on the rump, and Tillie bucked and began to gallop, with the Indian leading her. The others surrounded the buggy. The air was thick with dust as Elizabeth twisted around to look behind them.

"Charlie, run!" she screamed.

The buggy veered off the road, careening northward, and she saw Charlie pick himself up and begin to run. *Oh, God, don't let them go back for him.* She clung to the swaying sides of the buggy, wondering if she could jump out, but they were going too fast, and there were Indians all around her.

She sat back, bracing herself against the sway of the buggy, and tried to still her terror and think straight. The only Indians around here were Sioux, Ryan had said, but not all of them were Black Wolf's men. Black Wolf was having trouble controlling his young braves, because the white men kept provoking fights. All the lurid tales she had heard about Indians passed through her mind in grisly detail. She looked back and could still see Charlie, a small figure on the empty prairie.

"Boy's running off," one of the Indians shouted.

"Well, I don't want him," another shouted back.

They don't sound like Black Wolf's men, Elizabeth realized suddenly. She was alert now, no longer in a panic. As reason took over, she became suspicious, her eyes narrowing. She twisted around again and tried to see the leader, but he was well out of sight behind the back of the buggy. She looked at the horses galloping ahead of her. The flying hooves caught a flash of sunlight. Indians did not shoe their horses! Elizabeth sat up straight, her eyes glinting furiously.

She leaned out of the buggy, trying again to catch a glimpse of the leader, and saw beyond him a lone rider far behind them—a white man dogging their trail. Then the leader of the Indians dropped back and turned to lift his hand at the rider. As if on command, the rider spun his horse around and galloped toward Shawnee.

Elizabeth prayed briefly that he had gone for help, but her sharp senses, which had registered that wave of the hand, told her that he was involved with this band of supposed Indians. She was certain they were not Indians, but she found no comfort in that realization. Men who would abandon a nine-year-old boy in the middle of the prairie were capable of any cruelty.

"Look sharp!" the leader called out from behind.

Elizabeth stiffened. *There is something about that voice*. . . . Before she could pin it down, she saw riders approaching from the southwest. Cowboys! They rode straight at the buggy, howling and firing their guns.

The Indians fired back. The leader on the pinto horse shot his rifle while the other Indians clumsily shot bows and arrows. Elizabeth cowered on the buggy floor. Suddenly the Indians spun their mounts away from the buggy and galloped toward the northeast, leaving Tillie to bolt unchecked over the rocky ground.

The cowboys gave chase. As they caught up to her, Elizabeth picked herself up off the buggy floor with an expression of grim fury on her lips. She was not at all surprised when the cowboy who grabbed Tillie's reins and brought her to a halt turned out to be George Bigelow.

"Elizabeth!" Bigelow leaped off his horse and jumped into the buggy beside her. "Thank God you're safe!"

Outraged, Elizabeth started to confront Bigelow with her suspicions but quickly thought better of it. She realized that she was alone in the middle of the prairie with him and five of his ranch hands. Bigelow had done so many cruel, ruthless things that she was unsure what he might do to her if she crossed him. So she summoned the most grateful smile she could manage.

"I'm all right. Quite unharmed," she said. "But they put Charlie out of the buggy miles back. I've got to go find him."

"Charlie!" Bigelow looked irritated, but he patted her hand solicitously. "Certainly not, my dear. You need to rest and recover from this horrible experience. I'm going to take you to the Double X. It's not far from here. It's lucky we were out checking stock and saw those heathens in time. I'll send a couple of my boys for young Charlie."

Elizabeth considered that. She had no idea what Bigelow was up to, but everything was too coincidental. She would go along until she saw clearly what he was plotting.

"Very well, but please tell them to hurry. I won't rest until I know he's all right."

"You hear that?" Bigelow said over his shoulder.

Two of the cowboys rode off at a gallop in the direction the buggy had come. Bigelow shouted at a third to take Tillie's cut reins, and the buggy swung slowly around and set out toward the Double X. The other two riders followed, trailing Bigelow's horse.

Bigelow leaned back in the buggy and pulled his hat down over his eyes to block the sun. He smiled at Elizabeth. "You're a very lucky woman, my dear. The Sioux like white women for their squaws."

They made the rest of the drive in silence, each wrapped in private thoughts. George Bigelow mulled over a few more Indian horror stories in case Elizabeth Bradley was not suitably grateful for her rescue.

Elizabeth began to sort out the morning's events: the

"Indians," the pinto pony, the signal to the lone rider. She remembered the tension at the Fourth of July celebration and the rumors of Indian attack. *He's using me to start a war!* she realized, and wondered how she could get a message to Tim Ryan before someone told him about the Indians.

When they arrived at the Double X, Bigelow bowed and guided her ceremoniously into the house. The Double X ranch house was larger than Ryan's, and more elaborate, full of dark polished mahogany furniture. In the dining room, an elegant luncheon had been laid. For two, Elizabeth noted. Now it all made sense.

"I hope you'll have something to refresh yourself," Bigelow said.

Angrily, Elizabeth looked at the two plates, her eyes flashing. "I'm not hungry."

"That's a shame," Bigelow said cheerfully. "You need to keep up your strength after such a harrowing time. I've really gone to a great deal of trouble. You can't say I don't woo a woman properly."

Elizabeth's eyes opened wide. "I think you've lost your mind."

"On the contrary," Bigelow said, filling a plate with sliced ham and a piece of cake. "I am a man who knows what he wants. I generally get what I want. In this case, you'll be glad I did. You just haven't thought it out properly." He handed her the plate. "When you've eaten something, you won't be so overwrought."

Elizabeth put the plate down on the table with a thump. "I am not overwrought." She stifled an insane laugh. She had known that George Bigelow was dangerous, but she had not thought that he would carry it this far.

"It's perfectly natural to be upset," he said. "Any woman would be, after what you've been through. I have heard of women who were abducted by Indians losing their wits entirely. You are lucky we found you in time. The savages didn't—?" He paused delicately, but the expression in his eyes was not comforting; it was hard and calculating.

"I am unraped, if that's what you mean," Elizabeth snapped.

"I'm relieved to hear it," Bigelow said. "Of course, no

one else will believe it. People always like to think the worst. And after that little scene last night, I'm afraid your reputation isn't going to stand the strain." He cut himself a slice of ham. "Ruined is ruined, I'm afraid. You're really going to have to marry me. No one will have the temerity to gossip about my wife."

Elizabeth glared at him across the table. "I'd just as soon marry General Sherman," she told him, casting about for the worst person she could think of.

George Bigelow did not seem particularly insulted. "This is very good ham," he went on. "And you're going to have to eat sometime."

"Never!" Elizabeth snarled at him. She felt that if she ate the devil's food, she would somehow be tied to him. "And I want my son!"

"Oh, I expect they'll find him," Bigelow said. "I can't say I much want him, but if it will help you to see reason . . ."

Charlie picked himself up off the ground, his hands and knees stinging where they had hit the rutted trail. He could hear his mother screaming at him to run, but he hesitated. He wanted very much to run—he was terrified—but he knew that a brave person would go after those men instead and try to get his mother back. Charlie looked at the horses circling around the buggy. There were too many of them.

"Run!" his mother shouted again, and Charlie turned and ran. When he looked over his shoulder, the buggy and the horses were going the other way. Charlie choked back a sob and turned around and ran again. He had to find help, some grown men with horses and guns. He thought he might be closer to Shawnee than to home, but he did not know whom he could trust in Shawnee. For Charlie had seen real Indians up close, and he knew those men were not Indians. He also knew who rode that pinto horse—Charlie loved horses and knew every one of them on the Broken R—and he was probably more afraid of Cal Hodges than he would have been of any Indians.

He looked at the sun and the mountains, trying to judge

the direction. He was nearly ten miles from home, but there was someone he could trust who was closer than that, if he could just find the way. Monty Lang was Tim Ryan's friend, and Monty Lang would have nothing to do with Cal Hodges. Cal Hodges was angry at his mother about last night, Charlie thought, and he was concerned about what Cal Hodges might do to her. He had to find someone to stop him.

Charlie stumbled along desperately, looking for the track that led to Monty Lang's place.

It was hot now. The sun was beating down on his head, and he had left his hat in the buggy. His high-button shoes made running difficult. After half a mile, Charlie slowed to a walk, gasping for breath. He looked around him at the openness of the prairie.

A harsh, dry rattling sound from behind a rock froze him in his tracks. Charlie backed away carefully, his heart thumping. Against the dirt, he could just see the dull brown coils of the snake and the diamond pattern on its back. Its triangular head was half raised, and it buzzed menacingly. Charlie made a wide circle around it. The snake did not move. He walked on, looking fearfully over his shoulder, and then he glanced quickly ahead of him, in case more snakes were hidden, dull brown against the dry ground. His mouth was parched with thirst, but he hurried on.

Emma Lang was hanging wash on the line when she saw a small, dirty figure trudging down the track to the corral gate. She dropped the armful of clean petticoats into the basket at her feet and flew to meet him.

"Charlie? Honey, what happened to you?" She turned toward the house and shouted for Monty. Then she picked up the child and staggered toward the porch. He was nearly as big as she was and clung to her like a dead weight.

Monty came out with a bucket of water and a dipper, took one look at Charlie, and poured the first dipperful over his head. Leaning against Emma, Charlie drank the second dipperful and told them what had happened. Tears, dirt, and water flowed down his cheeks.

"We better get you home, young 'un," Monty said. "I can't go after those men by myself. Anyway, Tim Ryan'll skin me if I don't tell him first. I knew that Cal was bad news. Damn it, I told Tim he was. You sure it was Cal Hodges?"

Charlie nodded. "I'm sure. It was Cal's horse. And Mr. Ryan took me to see Indians." He frowned scornfully. "Those weren't Indians."

"You leave him here," Emma said firmly. She had pulled Charlie's shoes and stockings off and was washing his feet. "His poor feet are blistered raw, and he's half dead with this heat." She cuddled Charlie into her arm. "Don't you worry, honey. Monty and Mr. Ryan'll get your mama."

Monty looked at the exhausted child. "I reckon you're right," he told Emma. "All right, son, you tell me real careful which way they all went. Think hard where the sun was, and give me a good picture."

"Cal Hodges couldn't round up five men to dress up like Indians and pull off a stunt like that without some help." Tim Ryan was buckling on a gun belt with a Colt revolver in the holster as he spoke. "Somebody had a good reason for wanting them to look like Indians, and I know which son of a bitch that somebody was!" He picked up a rifle and slapped it into the case on his saddle.

"I thought so, too," Monty said. His eyes were grim. "But I thought maybe my opinion was just personal prejudice. Are you sure?"

"I've got about as personal a prejudice as you can get against George Bigelow," Ryan said, "and I aim to prove I'm right this time." Every cowhand who was not out with the stock was saddling up while the two men spoke. "If Bigelow wants war, he's getting one!"

"I doubt he wanted that," Monty said. "He was counting on a couple of green easterners being fooled. I doubt he'd try that stunt with Shawnee folk, but he's probably thinking he's pretty smart, picking on Mrs. Bradley and her boy."

"If he's scared her, I'll kill him," Ryan muttered.

"You better worry about why he did it," Monty said. "The Sioux are touchy right now. If some damn fools from town go out after them, the Sioux'll fight back. You and your friend Black Wolf won't have a prayer of stopping them. Bigelow must be crazy. What the hell's he after?"

"Land, the greedy bastard," Ryan said. "He's willing to start an Indian war and get half this town killed just to open up the Sioux grazing land. If he can make the Sioux start a war, the cavalry will do the rest for him."

"How are you gonna stop it?"

"I sent John Potter to Black Wolf," Ryan said. "Black Wolf trusts John. Maybe he can persuade 'em to lay low till I settle with Bigelow. I'm not going to have Elizabeth in the middle of this."

Elizabeth? Monty cocked an eye at Ryan, wondering just how much she figured in Ryan's outrage.

Ryan swung into his saddle while Beau, sensing his rider's mood, pranced nervously.

Monty mounted up beside him. "Well, just try to keep in mind that you ain't gonna do Mrs. Bradley any good if they hang you for murdering George Bigelow."

Joe Sipes had worked for George Bigelow for years, and he had learned to survive. The boss let nothing stand in the way of what he wanted, and if Joe wanted to go on working for the Double X, he had better follow the boss's orders to the letter without arguing. All the same, as he rode into Shawnee at a dead gallop, just as Bigelow had told him, he felt like a damn fool.

"Injuns!" Joe hollered as he rode down the main street.

Sheriff Hank Purchase came galumphing down the street, buckling his gun belt. The Sawyer House door flew open, and ladies popped out of Fishburn's.

"Injuns!" Joe screamed again. "They was leading Mrs. Bradley's buggy, and they had Mrs. Bradley in it! Heading north! I'd have followed them, but there was too many of 'em. I hung back just long enough to see which way they was going. We gotta go after them! We gotta get a posse!"

"You sure it was Mrs. Bradley?" Hank said.

"Hell, yes. I saw all that yellow hair flyin' out. She was screamin' blue murder, and one of them heathens was holdin' her down in the buggy."

"Right," Hank said. "You head down to Meg Callahan's—that's the quickest way to find enough men. I'll saddle up and meet you back here."

Twenty minutes later, the street was a seething throng of mounted men, buggies, and wagons. Those who did not live in Shawnee wanted to go home and protect their households, although few were inclined to go do it alone. One Indian raid might well mean that another was coming, or it might be a ruse to draw the men out of the town. Sheriff Purchase was trying to get them into some kind of order.

"Let's get those devils!" Joe Sipes yelled, pleased with the stir he had caused. "This time they've gone too far!"

"If you go tearing off into Sioux country like a stampede," Robert Cummings yelled back, "you'll put Mrs. Bradley in more danger. There aren't enough of us to tackle the Sioux. We've got to leave some men in town!" He was sitting in his buggy, having returned from a leisurely drive with his wife to find the town in an uproar. Lily clutched his arm, her face white.

"This ain't no time for caution," a cowboy shouted back. "They been asking for it!" Eager for a fight, he spun his horse around. "Let's get 'em!"

"You're Bigelow's man, aren't you?" Robert Cummings asked Joe. "We'll pick up the men at his place, and then go on and get more at Tim Ryan's. Tim knows the Indians better than anybody. Dad—" He looked at Dad Henry. "You bring your boys back into town to keep watch here."

"We ain't got time!" Joe Sipes said. "Who knows what they're doin' to that poor woman right now?"

Meg Callahan had climbed into her landau and followed her customers along the main street. "If they're gonna rape her, they've done it already," she said flatly. "And they aren't gonna kill her, or they'd have done that when they caught her." She edged her buggy forward. "And you aren't gonna go off and leave this town with no protection, Joe Sipes. You pick up some men at Bigelow's."

"I told you, he don't want—damn it, I mean he ain't

even there," Joe said. "And we ain't got the time. You want Bigelow and Ryan so bad, you go get 'em."

Meg's eyes narrowed. She did not trust George Bigelow or any man who worked for him. If Joe Sipes did not want Bigelow or Ryan along, then Bigelow was up to something, she was sure of it. So she looked around at the rest of the crowd in the street.

"You all gonna let this idiot talk you into riding out there after those heathen Sioux without enough men? Bigelow's hands will double the size of your posse. Give you a fighting chance."

"We ain't got time!" Joe said again, looking nervous.

"Who's the sheriff here, Hank?" Meg said. "You or this cowboy?"

Hank Purchase straightened his gun belt. "I am. And we're going to Bigelow's."

"Hank!" Joe Sipes yelped. "You don't understand—"

It was too late. Everybody else was yelling their agreement. Joe Sipes could get shot by himself if he wanted to. They were getting some reinforcements first.

Meg Callahan looked grimly after them as the mounted men thundered out of town toward the Double X. Joe Sipes was beating his horse on the flanks with his hat and was spurring him hard, trying to outdistance them. Something fishy was going on at Bigelow's, Meg was sure. George Bigelow was most likely at home and in for a surprise. She picked up the big Colt she had laid on the seat of the landau, put it in her lap, and shook the reins.

As Meg's carriage took off, Lily looked fearfully at Robert. "I'm going with you," she said. "I have to know what's happened to Elizabeth."

"What about the children?"

"They're at Agnes Sawyer's," Lily said. "They'll be all right. Bobby's old enough to watch the young ones. Robert, come on!"

As the posse, with its trail of buggies and wagons behind it, thundered out of town, the stage from Cheyenne pulled in. Federal Marshal Evans Carrington alighted, with his carpetbag in his hand and his badge pinned on his vest, and cocked an eye at the ruckus in the street. He went inside the depot and leaned his elbows on the telegraph operator's counter. "Mind telling me what in the hell is going on here?"

Elizabeth Bradley faced George Bigelow across the imported Limoges dinnerware on his dining room table. The slice of ham he had cut for her was beginning to curl at the edges, and the ice—brought from the mountains at considerable trouble—packed around the fruit salad was melting and dripping on the tablecloth. Altogether it was a dispirited-looking meal that had thoroughly failed to serve its host's purpose, that of demonstrating to Elizabeth Bradley the elegant life she would lead as Mrs. George Bigelow.

It was a depressing dining room anyway, Elizabeth thought, full of dark mahogany paneling and still-life paintings of fruit and dead game. In one, a brace of freshly killed rabbits lay on a table beside a bowl of pears. It was an art style that had never appealed to Elizabeth, especially in a dining room. Over the fireplace was a framed pair of silver-mounted pistols, as if the master of the house might suddenly wish to go out and shoot a rabbit to paint. Elizabeth thought she would rather go hungry than sit down to dinner every night looking at those paintings.

George Bigelow sat at the head of the table, arms crossed, looking at her with amusement. "Your gratitude is overwhelming," he remarked.

"I'm not grateful to be kidnapped by a lunatic!" Elizabeth snapped at him. "Who would be? I know perfectly well those weren't Indians."

"They'll be Indian enough for everyone else," Bigelow said. "You try saying they weren't, and folks will just think you don't want to admit it because you're afraid word will get around that you were raped."

"If there's any rape going on, it looks more to me as if you were planning it here," Elizabeth said, not even bothering to be shocked at the word.

"Nothing of the sort," Bigelow said. "I am never so crude. I had just planned on your spending the night here if you proved to be, uh, recalcitrant. That ought to do the trick just as well."

"You wouldn't dare!"

"Oh, wouldn't I? Everybody thinks you're being dragged off by your hair into some Sioux's teepee thirty miles from here. Who is going to come and take you home?"

"You are," Elizabeth said grimly. "If you don't give me my buggy back, I'll make such a fuss you won't be able to hold your head up in Wyoming Territory again!"

Bigelow laughed scornfully. "I doubt that the ravings of an hysterical woman, rescued from savages, would be given much credence against the word of her rescuer."

"Rescuer! You mean kidnapper! And I don't believe for a minute your men went to find Charlie. You left him out there on the prairie by himself, and I am going to go get my son." She snatched one of the pistols from its frame over the mantelpiece and leveled it at him. "I'll settle with you when I've found him."

Bigelow chuckled. "That isn't loaded."

"Are you sure? I've never known anyone in this heathen territory who kept a gun that wasn't loaded," she said. "How badly do you want to find out?" She aimed the pistol very carefully at a spot just below his trouser buttons.

Bigelow fidgeted in his chair. He had heard that southern ladies were delicate and sensitive, but Elizabeth Bradley was not living up to that reputation. Since he had told his men to stay away from the house, none of them were within earshot to come to his assistance, and he knew he could not get to his loaded rifle in the next room while Elizabeth held the pistol on him. Bigelow shuddered.

"Now, Elizabeth—" he said, soothingly.

She pulled the hammer back.

The sound of footsteps running along the veranda outside startled them. Elizabeth quickly slipped the gun in the folds of her skirt as Cal Hodges threw the dining room door open. He had changed out of his Indian disguise, and Bigelow greeted him with a mixture of relief and irritation.

"I thought I told you to stay out," Bigelow snapped.

"Ryan's on his way!" Cal hurried across the dining room to Bigelow, ignoring Elizabeth. "I don't know how he found out, but—"

"Goddamn it!" Bigelow said. "Keep him out of here!"

As he spoke there were more running footsteps, and suddenly Tim Ryan stood framed in the dining room door, staring angrily at them. Cal Hodges whirled, drawing his gun as he spun, and fired at Ryan.

The bullet spat past Ryan's ear and buried itself in the paneling.

"No!" Elizabeth shrieked. She raised the little silver pistol and fired at Cal Hodges in the same instant that Tim Ryan aimed his Colt revolver. The recoiling gun bucked in her hand, driving her fist and the hammer back into her face.

Cal crumpled as the Colt's bullet whined over his falling body.

Elizabeth, still holding the pistol, stared in horror at Cal Hodges, saw his body twitch once and lie still. There was a hole and a spreading pool of blood in his chest. Her face was numb from the blow of the hammer, and she could feel blood trickling into her mouth.

All motion in the room stopped. She bent and touched Cal's body. He was dead.

Chapter Twelve

Tim Ryan crossed the room in two strides and gathered Elizabeth in his arms. Sobbing, she buried her face in his shoulder, the pistol still clenched in her fingers.

"It's all right," he said gently. "You're all right."

"I killed him," she sobbed. "Oh, God, I didn't mean to kill him."

"Nah, you didn't kill him," Ryan said. He loosened the gun from her fingers. "I killed him." He would have, if she had not fired first. His conscience could stand the knowledge better than hers. "You missed him, honest you did." He gave George Bigelow a look that said that if he denied it, he would be the next one shot.

Elizabeth's sobs abated a little.

"Charlie's all right," Ryan added. "He's at Monty Lang's place. What is going on here?" He looked with suspicion at the congealing luncheon and George Bigelow's Limoges dinnerware.

Elizabeth sniffled, averting her eyes from Cal Hodges's body. "How did you know to look for me here?"

"Because your boy knows a fake Indian when he sees one. Bigelow, if you've done her any harm—"

"No harm at all," Bigelow said, airily ignoring Cal's body. "My intentions were entirely honorable. In fact, they still are. And perhaps Mrs. Bradley should reconsider them, in case there's any, uh, question over who shot whom."

"He was going to make me stay here until I said I'd marry him," Elizabeth said. "Until everyone thought I was ruined, and I had to."

"Do give it some more thought," Bigelow said conversationally. "A corpse in the parlor should only add to your already interesting reputation."

"You shut up, Bigelow!" Ryan snarled at him.

"I appreciate the honor you have done me, Mr. Bigelow," Elizabeth said sarcastically, "but since I am planning to leave Shawnee, it won't be necessary for me to marry anyone."

"The hell you are," Ryan said. "You aren't that ruined. Anyway, I ruined you first, so you just stay here and marry me."

"Mister Ryan!"

Bigelow gave a hoot of laughter.

Ryan gently turned Elizabeth to him and looked into her eyes. "I'm sorry; that wasn't the best way to put it. I love you. I've known that since last night, but you were so mad at me. I was gonna court you for a while—take you to church and pick you flowers and so on. But maybe this fool is right." He jerked a thumb at Bigelow. "It'll save a lot of talk if you just marry me now."

Elizabeth looked at him searchingly. He meant it. She could see it in those ruefully honest green eyes. She leaned her head wearily against his shoulder and sighed with relief.

"All right," she agreed softly.

"Mr. Ryan is forgetting one point," Bigelow said. "He is not in a position to marry anybody. I regret to disillusion you, my dear, but the lovely Caroline didn't die of cholera. She left him." He gave Elizabeth a wolfish smile. "As a matter of fact, she ran off with my foreman and is no doubt living a life of pleasant sin in San Francisco even now. Of course, you could always move to Utah. I believe the Mormons allow any number of wives."

Elizabeth started to inform him that she knew about Caroline, but Ryan forestalled her. In one motion he released Elizabeth and grabbed George Bigelow by the collar. As Bigelow raised his arm to defend himself, Ryan's fist slammed into his chin. Bigelow crashed onto the dining room table, smashed into the soup tureen, and rolled to the floor.

Joe Sipes, hurtling through the door to tell his boss that the posse had strayed from its intended path and was hot on his heels, skidded to a halt and goggled at him. His eyes opened even wider when he saw Cal Hodges.

"That's Cal Hodges," Joe informed Bigelow, as if Bigelow might not have noticed the body on his rug. "You shoot him, boss?"

"No." The word emerged as a groan. Bigelow painfully wiped the soup off his face.

"Well, that's good," Joe said, "because there's a posse right behind me. I tried to turn 'em around, boss, but that busybody whore got 'em all worked up about not having enough men to tackle the Injuns, and I couldn't get Hank Purchase off to one side in time."

"You half-wit," Bigelow groaned. He struggled up to a sitting position, soup dripping thickly down his shirt-front.

"The yard's fulla of Ryan's men, too," Joe added. He jerked his thumb at Ryan curiously. "Did he shoot him?"

"Never mind who shot him," Bigelow said. "Just get that posse out of here."

"Well, he wasn't no loss," Joe said. "I was just interested, that's all."

"Get them out of here!" Bigelow said, heaving himself to his feet.

"That ain't going to be easy," Joe said. "There's Injuns coming, too. Real ones," he added.

Tim Ryan sprinted for the door.

Joe Sipes looked out the window. "Don't look like our boys stood up too good to Ryan's men. And there's a federal marshal out there, too," he told Bigelow.

"Oh, God." George Bigelow staggered out the door behind Ryan.

*   *   *

Federal Marshal Evans Carrington drew his horse to a halt and surveyed the scene. It was the damnedest thing he had ever seen. The posse was drawn up outside George Bigelow's ranch house, about a hundred yards from the front door. The intervening space was filled with a smaller group of horsemen, who had herded a bunch of cowboys into the center of the ranch yard. Behind the posse, what looked like half the town of Shawnee was milling around Carrington. Buggies, buckboards, farmers on mules, and a painted lady in a landau who was either a high-priced whore or an actress. More were coming. Two barefoot boys in overalls galumphed up on a plow horse as Carrington sat there. A gray-haired woman in a buckboard spotted them and swung around.

"You, Clem and Johnny, you get home before I take a switch to you!"

"Aw, Ma, we want to see them fight the Injuns!"

Carrington narrowed his eyes and pulled a pair of field glasses from the saddlebag on his livery-stable mount. Beyond the ranch house, on the other side of a little bowl of a valley, another line of horsemen had drawn up. Carrington peered at them. Sioux, he thought, just sitting there, quietly.

Carrington swung his field glasses back to the knot of horsemen in the yard. All their mounts, Carrington noted, had a Broken R brand. They did not seem concerned about the Indians. They were giving all their attention to the cowboys on the ground, keeping them herded together like a bunch of sheep.

Carrington shook his head. In twenty years of employed and freehand law enforcement, he had never seen anything like it. Well, Tim Ryan had called in a federal marshal to sort things out, and Carrington was going to sort them. He pushed his horse forward through the crowd.

As he got to the front of the posse, he saw a big square man wearing a sheriff's badge and looking uneasy. As well he might, Carrington snorted.

"Carrington, federal marshal's office," he said briskly. "What in the blazes do you think you're doing here?"

Sheriff Hank Purchase turned to look at him. "Oh, Lord," he moaned.

"Where's Timothy Ryan?" Carrington demanded.

Purchase looked toward the house. "Down there, I reckon," he sighed.

Through the open front door of George Bigelow's house came two men, one of them holding his jaw gingerly. His shirtfront was a mess of stains. The second man, a tanned, wiry cowboy, was shouting.

"Bigelow, you call that posse off or I'll break every bone in your lying body!"

"You get your Indians out of here, Ryan, or we'll clear that rangeland ourselves," Bigelow said thickly.

"Get those heathen!" somebody in the posse shouted.

Across the empty bowl of land, the line of Indians stirred, and Carrington saw raised rifles.

"That does it," Carrington muttered. He straightened his vest front so the marshal's badge showed clearly. Then he drew his pistol and fired it into the air.

"Now you all listen to me! I'm a federal marshal and nobody's starting a fight in federal land!" He cupped his hands to his mouth. "And you Sioux clear out! Go home and there won't be any trouble."

The Sioux did not move, and Carrington could hear another quiet stir as rifles were lifted nearby.

"They stole a white woman," someone shouted.

A chorus of angry voices rose to express their outrage. The posse raised its rifles, too, and the horseless men in the ranch yard dived for cover.

"Hold your fire!" Ryan shouted.

"Who are you?" Carrington bellowed at him.

"I'm Tim Ryan," Ryan shouted back. "And the woman's in the house here, so make those idiots in the posse put their guns down."

"And let those heathen murder us in cold blood?" a man in the posse yelled.

"If the woman's all right, ain't nothing to hold us back. I say we get 'em!" another called out in agreement.

Carrington spurred his horse out in front of the posse and faced them, pistol in one hand and a shotgun in the other. His back was to the Sioux. "Ryan!" he yelled. "If you got something to say, say it!"

There was no answer. Carrington spun his head around, but Ryan was gone.

"Look! There he is!"

Ryan staggered through the door of the ranch house with a body slung over his shoulder. He heaved it over the back of his horse and, with a slap on the horse's rump, sent it trotting toward the posse. "There's your Indian!" he shouted.

Then he turned his back and walked slowly across the empty valley toward the Sioux. There was no gun in his hand. The Sioux aimed their rifles at him, but at a half-heard command from their leader, they lowered them slowly, watchfully. The sun glinted on the long barrels.

"Come back!" Carrington shouted, but Ryan shook his head. Carrington dismounted and bent to look at the body that slid from Ryan's big roan horse.

Ryan kept walking. If there were any chance of averting a war now, only he and Black Wolf could do it. If they were unsuccessful, war would spread from Shawnee through the rest of Wyoming Territory. George Bigelow would have his northern rangeland, and white men and Indians alike would have countless dead to mourn. Tim Ryan cursed Bigelow as he walked.

"What are you doing here, my friend?" he said to Black Wolf when he was close enough to speak without the other white men hearing him. The Indians' grim faces were painted for war, and the younger braves looked restless, hungry for fighting.

"Your man John Potter came to us to ask that we lie low," Black Wolf said somberly. "My young braves will not lie low, not anymore. I am their chieftain, so I came. We do not wait any longer and hope that the white man will treat us fairly. The white man has raised a war band against us."

"Not the white man," Ryan said. "One white man. I know that if the men of Black Wolf were going to steal a white woman, it would not be Elizabeth Bradley. I saw you mark her for your protection in your camp.

Now the other white men know it, too. I have proved it to them."

"How?" Black Wolf asked. "They have not listened to you before. No, the time has come that we knew was on the trail—the time for the choosing of sides."

Ryan, knowing how vulnerable he was, stood carefully, eyeing the Indians' guns. "I have given them the man who dressed himself as a Sioux to bring evil repute on your tribe," he said. He pointed back across the empty land at the body of Cal Hodges, lying next to his horse, and the men clustered at the body. "There were still traces of the war paint in his hair. He is dead now, and now they know."

Black Wolf spoke quickly to his men. Some nodded their heads, but others looked angrier than before.

"Where is John Potter?" Ryan said quietly.

"He is in our camp," Black Wolf said. "If we win this battle, we will let him go."

"And if you lose?" Ryan said.

Black Wolf shrugged.

Ryan thought rapidly. If the Sioux men fought and lost, the Sioux women would take out their vengeance on John Potter. "Take me instead," he said. "I am the one who sent him to you. Take me and let him go."

Black Wolf shook his head. "That is not your destiny. Your destiny is to take your side with your people. I will not rob you of that. John Potter is nothing to me."

"My destiny will catch me when it will," Ryan said. "But it is not time. There is no need for war now, not with the men of Shawnee. If you will go now, and free John Potter, there will be no fight or further insult offered you. I swear it."

Black Wolf turned to his men, speaking slowly and evenly, while Ryan waited. He turned back to Ryan, ready to speak, but Ryan never heard what he was going to say. A shot rang out, and the young brave beside Black Wolf dropped from his pony, writhing in the dirt.

Tim Ryan spun around and saw the glint of a gun barrel in the ranch house window. He leapt up and yanked Black Wolf from his horse. They wrestled together in the dirt momentarily, until Ryan heard a woman's scream from the house. In terror for Elizabeth, Ryan swiftly pinned Black Wolf to the ground and covered the Indian's body with his own. Another shot went over their heads.

"Don't move," Ryan gasped. "He's aiming at you."

The Indians around them had raised their rifles again, some of them dismounting and aiming at Ryan. Black Wolf spat dirt from his mouth and barked a sharp command just before one brave was about to leap on Tim Ryan. The Indians waited, barely in check. Ryan could feel the long cold barrels pointed at his back. A bolt clicked.

"Don't shoot! Any of you!" a woman's voice screamed. "No! Don't shoot!"

Ryan let go of Black Wolf and rolled over. In the front window of the ranch house, lit by dusty sunlight, he saw George Bigelow nursing what appeared to be a broken wrist. Elizabeth stood beside him, a poker in her hand. A rifle lay on the porch floor outside the window.

"We will go now," Black Wolf said. He was mounted, the wounded brave beside him with a tourniquet around his leg. "There is a life between us now, Tim Ryan. It has brought us both peace for a time. Maybe only for today. But I will send John Potter back to you."

"Will I see you again?" Ryan said.

"I do not know," Black Wolf said somberly. "The time for choosing sides is still on the trail. It will still come. I do not know," he said again. He spun his pony around, and the Sioux galloped behind him, fanning out as they rode, spreading out across the land.

Ryan turned and walked slowly toward George Bigelow's house.

Inside, he found Lily Cummings and Marshal Carrington tending to Elizabeth and Bigelow in the dining room. George Bigelow stood gritting his teeth while Carrington taped his wrist. Lily Cummings was cleaning Elizabeth's bloodied face with her handkerchief, moistened with melted ice from the table. There was a deep gash on Elizabeth's upper lip.

"Are you all right?" Ryan asked her.

Elizabeth nodded.

He sat down on a chair beside her, relieved. "You're lucky you didn't lose your front teeth," he muttered. "Don't you know to keep your arm straight?"

"I do now," she said, holding a piece of ice to her lip.

Lily looked at Ryan with exasperation.

"You just stay out of it, Lily," Ryan said. "I'll conduct my romances my own way."

Elizabeth chuckled affectionately and put her hand on his shoulder. Ryan took it in his.

In the corner, Joe Sipes was trying his best to disassociate himself from the day's events, explaining to Hank Purchase that he had had no idea what was going on.

Hank Purchase did not believe him. Hank was smart enough—and enough of an opportunist—to know that George Bigelow was finished in Shawnee. He turned to Elizabeth with respect. "You want to press charges against him?" Hank jerked his thumb at Bigelow.

Elizabeth turned her attention away from Ryan for a moment. "I don't know," she said. She looked back to Ryan. She knew they both would be the center of attention at a trial, and she was reluctant to expose them to such scandal. The truth about Caroline would come out, and then the twins would know and be hurt. All Ryan's efforts to protect the girls would be undone.

"Depends on how vengeful you feel," Ryan murmured.

"I'll decide in the morning," Elizabeth said. She already knew that in the morning she would tell Hank Purchase to let Bigelow go. In the meantime, a night in jail would be very good for him.

Evans Carrington looked at her with respect. He sensed her intention and heartily approved. "You take your time," he suggested. He glanced at Ryan. "However, there's a dead man out there that hasn't been accounted for."

Tim Ryan stood up wearily and raised Elizabeth up from her chair. "He shot first, and I killed him," Ryan said. "This lady was there. We'll be glad to sign a statement when you want one."

"I'll want one," Carrington said.

"Just don't wait too long," Ryan said. "I've got a honey-moon planned, and I don't want it interfered with." He took Elizabeth's hand and led her out of the house.

In the yard, people were still milling about, asking each other what was happening and offering opinions. When they saw Ryan and Elizabeth, they converged on them.

Ryan waved them away. "Ask Hank," he said. "He knows more than he usually does." Pony Simkins had brought Elizabeth's buggy out of the barn, and Ryan helped her into it and then got in beside her. As he did, he saw Meg's landau, standing away from the rest. He started to call something to her, but she just gave him a wave with a half-lifted hand and turned toward town.

Ryan sighed. He knew it was good-bye. He had said too many good-byes today. Bigelow's downfall would buy the Sioux some time, but he doubted he would see Black Wolf again. Too many good-byes. . . . But there was one, the most important one, that would not be said now. He put his arm around Elizabeth and gently pressed her head to his shoulder as Tillie, her cut reins tied, clip-clopped toward the Broken R.

It was, as everyone said afterward, a humdinger of a wedding. Now that he was sure Elizabeth was going to marry him, Ryan had raised no objections when Lily Cummings took charge and orchestrated the whole affair. He would have preferred to marry Elizabeth immediately, but Lily declared that if Elizabeth and he were going to stay in Shawnee, Ryan would have to act respectably. Realizing that Lily was right, he had agreed when she made Elizabeth stay in town with her for the two weeks before the wedding.

When the big day had finally arrived, everyone, including Ryan, thought it had been worth the wait. Lily and Robert Cummings stood up for the couple, and Charlie, in a new suit, gave the bride away. Elizabeth's ethereal blonde beauty and joyous expression would have befitted an eighteen-year-old bride. She wore a new blue silk dress, appropriate for a bride at her second wedding. The twins were flower girls, scattering the same wildflowers as those in the bride's bouquet. The Reverend Mr. William Leslie read the service, and nearly everyone in Shawnee was there, with the exception of George Bigelow, who had put his ranch up for sale and moved.

Elizabeth had graciously sent Meg Callahan an invitation—much to the scandal of the ladies who knew about it. But with Tim Ryan about to put his ring on her finger, Elizabeth could afford to be generous. She had heard how Meg had contrived to send the posse to the Double X, and she was grateful.

Meg, who Lily Cummings said thankfully had more sense than Elizabeth, had discreetly declined but had sent a silver bowl as a wedding present.

The town hall was decked out as never before for the reception. Pink and white streamers hung from the beams, and baskets of wildflowers were arranged in corners and on tables. The wedding presents were displayed on a table covered with Lily's second-best tablecloth.

Elizabeth had been reluctant to display the gifts and put on such a show of grandeur, but Lily had said that everyone in town would be dying to know what the presents were and Elizabeth had best let them satisfy their curiosity.

Emma Lang had given them a blue and white quilt of truly exquisite workmanship, and Lily and Robert Cummings a set of delicately flowered luncheon plates. Some of the other presents were considerably more unusual. Elvina Fishburn had given them a maroon pillow, cross-stitched with the somber motto, "Man that is born of a woman is of few days, and full of trouble." Dad Henry had sent a stuffed armadillo. "Just the thing for the parlor," Elizabeth had told him gallantly.

George Bigelow had sent a present, particularly for Elizabeth, he told her in the accompanying card, in case she should need to defend her virtue again: a pearl-handled pistol. Elizabeth had not displayed that. In fact she had had a good deal of trouble preventing Ryan from taking the pistol back to North Platte, whence it had come, and shooting George Bigelow with it. Instead, he had contented himself with buying the piece of Bigelow's land that bordered Monty Lang's spread and giving it to Monty and Emma as a belated wedding present of their own. He would hear no argument from Monty, who tried to protest Ryan's generosity.

Little Deer, supervised by Lily, had prepared a matchless feast of ham, roast venison, peas, apple cobbler, and damson pie. There was champagne sent from Cheyenne and packed in ice brought down from the mountains by John Potter and Monty Lang. Lily had arranged the bottles in a white iron bathtub. It was the only thing she had been able to find that was big enough, and it looked light-hearted and fanciful with pink ribbons tied around its feet.

After everyone had eaten as much ham and damson pie as they could, there was a band of fiddle music and Angus Ogilvie's bagpipes for dancing.

Ryan danced the first dance with Elizabeth, and the second and third with his daughters. Then, taking Elizabeth's hand and giving Lily, who was keeping the children for the night, a grin over his shoulder, he slipped out into the darkness with his bride. Their buggy was tied outside the town hall, decorated with pink bows. A sign reading Tied and Branded had been tacked on it; Ryan was sure it was Sam Harkness's handiwork. They climbed into the buggy and turned Jericho's nose toward the Broken R. They were going to Colorado Springs on the stagecoach for their honeymoon, but not until the children had been returned to the Broken R in Little Deer's charge and they had had a chance to say good-bye. For tonight the house was empty and all theirs.

Elizabeth leaned her head on Ryan's shoulder and looked up at the sky, stretching endlessly dark and star strewn above them. It was still big, but somehow it did not seem too big anymore, with the constellations riding in their familiar places. A wolf howled in the mountains, and a rabbit zoomed across the road under Jericho's feet, making him snort.

"Happy, Mrs. Ryan?" Tim said.

Elizabeth snuggled closer to him in answer, and he bent his head and kissed her. As she wrapped her arms around him and kissed him hungrily, he turned sideways in the buggy, his arms sliding around her waist. Jericho snorted again and waggled his ears as the reins slapped against first one side of his neck and then the other. Finally he came to a complete halt.

"Tim," Elizabeth said, when she could get her breath. "We've stopped."

Ryan chuckled. He wrapped the reins around the whipsocket and smacked Jericho on the rump. "The horse knows the way," he said. He put his arms around Elizabeth again as Jericho trotted toward the Broken R and home.

STAGECOACH

STATION 38:

GRAND TETON
by Hank Mitchum

The bloody Brubaugh gang has earned a reputation for heartless cruelty, and their assassination of Colorado's governor, followed by their abduction of two women, does nothing to improve it. Gavin Brubaugh, oldest son of the gang's ruthless leader, Ma Brubaugh, leads the men north toward their Wyoming hideout, where Ma has been waiting.

When the gang reaches the hideout, they learn that a large cash shipment will be traveling by stage the next day, heading for Jackson, and they make plans to rob it. After taking the money, they also take hostage the most beautiful woman they have ever seen. Jenny Moore is eager to reach Jackson, where she plans to marry Lobo Lincoln. When she is taken hostage, she fears her dreams will never come true.

Lobo Lincoln, a huge, muscular half-breed who has been a government agent, army scout, and buffalo hunter, is stunned to learn of Jenny's abduction. He immediately takes action, setting out to rescue the beautiful woman who is to be his wife. He chases the gang through the foothills of the Tetons, enduring an Indian attack that leaves him near death. Nothing will keep him from finding Jenny—and the Brubaughs soon learn that infuriating Lobo Lincoln is the same as committing suicide.

Read GRAND TETON, on sale November 1988 wherever Bantam paperbacks are sold.